LIFE ON HOLD

LIFE ON HOLD

Fahd al-Atiq

—⁂—

Translated by
Jonathan Wright

The American University in Cairo Press
Cairo   New York

First published in 2012 by
The American University in Cairo Press
113 Sharia Kasr el Aini, Cairo, Egypt
420 Fifth Avenue, New York, NY 10018
www.aucpress.com

Dar el Kutub No. 2254/12
ISBN 978 977 416 566 5

Dar el Kutub Cataloging-in-Publication Data

al-Atiq, Fahd
     Life on Hold / Fahd al-Atiq; translated by Fahd al-Atiq.—Cairo:
   The American University in Cairo Press, 2012
        p.   cm.
        ISBN 978 977 416 566 5
        1. English fiction   I. Title
        823

1 2 3 4 5   16 15 14 13 12

Designed by Andrea El-Akshar
Printed in Egypt

This book is dedicated to:

my daughter Ghada
and my son Badr
and the nomads of glorious Najd,
a modest attempt to come close to the creature on hold
    in all of us

Body and Soul

THE DAYS are all much alike here.

But drama class is preferable to drawing class.

Perhaps.

In drawing class at primary school, Khaled drew the face of a girl with a short plait. The teacher stood behind him and marked an X on the girl's neck.

That girl with the plait, she's the reason for his constant pangs of conscience. It was to her dark shadow that Khaled went one night, all eyes and fingers, to explore her young body. She was submissive, he was frightened, and neither of them knows what happened that night when her childhood danced. She danced on the threshold of something new, to shadowy, sensual music.

Once he drew a sun and a moon in the same picture.

The teacher laughed. "That never happens, my boy," he said.

—҈—

In the theater at university, Khaled acted in a foreign play with his colleagues. It was about big wolves that plunder the country. They closed the theater for maintenance. When he wrote about the pangs of conscience that made him ill, and sent what he wrote to the newspaper, they said it wasn't fit for publication because it was fictional.

The days are all much the same here.

The truth remains elusive.

Especially now, in this age, everything is in an elusive state.

In this city of masks, the days have been much the same in their tedium since distant times.

Even the faces look alike, and everyone looks aimlessly into the faces of others. But what is behind all these looks, all these masks?

He fell asleep while his uncle finished reading the poem by Ahmad Matar, "My Country Is a Blind Child," and in the morning the courtyard was covered in colored chalk scribblings. It was a fresh morning, and between the old walls you could hear the slow breathing of his family as they slept, their faces lit by the warm red sun. A child crawled across the floor in loose clothes.

Why do I love this place, why do I hate this place? He didn't know.

Khaled came out of the small room and saw the courtyard covered in chalk marks. He lay down next to the child that was crawling in loose clothes. The child, his sister Afaf, was like a cat, with long nails and disheveled hair and eyes that stared in wonder, darting from one thing to another.

On such a morning, a morning as strong as the pounding of his heart, he could absentmindedly forget his pangs of conscience. He tried to rest his head on Afaf's back, intending to sing her a sad song, but she turned away from him. He remembered the smell of her body—another thing from the past—like the smell of waking up, or the smell of stale urine. He went back to the question about the soul and the body.

"Come in, change your clothes and wash your face."

He would have liked to stay like that, like something suspended between heaven and earth, and cry. Why cry? He didn't know.

A fear aroused suspicions about everything.

Why fear?

When I sleep, I choke on my saliva and wake up in a panic, struggling to breathe. I drink a glass of water and go back to sleep.

Khaled got a dream job, but it turned into monotonous drudgery. From the moment he started work, and often thereafter, he would see his boss looking at his watch during meetings, while his boss's boss was busy with phone calls. They all seemed to be anxious, and eager to evade commitments. He started to sense that the job that had once seemed a dream was now collapsing in front of him. He felt frustrated. He dropped the precious thing he was holding and it broke into small fragments.

He tore out a page about his life that he had written one day in the university theater and hid it in the pocket of his best clothes. It was about a job he would find fulfilling, but the piece of paper turned into something else that had nothing to do with his old dreams.

His boss, who was also his relative, said: "Work hard so you'll be promoted and can retire on a good pension."

The advice shocked him.

But his father assured him: "That's advice from a man of experience."

That was when the fear began.

He began to have doubts about everything, sometimes just a pang of conscience, but one that shook his whole being.

He left that job, went on to another one, and later found out that his former boss had grown rich, had opened a private school, and had then become a consultant in the office of an important man.

Khaled finally settled down in a company, a new company full of engineers and Indian workers, but working there was chaotic and confusing. One afternoon, the manager had lunch brought for the engineers and workers—large platters of rice and chicken. They put the food on cloths on the floor in the middle of the main hall. Everyone ate, talking, squeezing lemon on everything, then drinking cola. When it was over, the manager took aside the engineer in charge and asked him to take care of the company, because he wanted to go abroad on vacation. The engineer asked him about the workers' salaries. Hurriedly he answered: "When I come back, my friend." He went to his car and one of the workers ran after him shouting, "Boss, boss!" "What do you want, Azim al-Zaman?" the manager asked. Azim said, "My salary, sir!" "Go see the engineers," he answered sharply. Then he screeched off in his car.

For several months, Khaled continued working in this new company with no manager. But one gloomy morning, he found the company wasn't there any longer. It was deserted. He asked the janitor at the building next door, and the janitor said, "I don't know." From the newspapers he learned that the engineer in charge had pilfered all the money and fled, and when the owner on vacation heard what had happened he had a stroke, so his vacation turned into a medical trip. As for Azim al-Zaman, he got a job as a driver in the house opposite the old company.

Khaled went back to his old government job, after giving up many of his dreams. He would turn up for work in the morning, sign the register, read the papers, chat with his colleagues, and they would laugh. Then he would think about how he might leave work early to go to sleep, or read and watch the daily serials on television.

The days are still all much the same here.

When he acted in his first play in the university theater, the faculty and his colleagues clapped. But when he graduated he couldn't find a stage to act on. He found a theater of the absurd in the details of his daily life, so he decided it was better to take part in this absurdity, rather than just be a spectator.

After this fantasy notion came to him, he gave up writing. His life gradually began to reach into areas that were new to him. He made new friends and a new life, and little by little he adopted a dissolute lifestyle. He would travel abroad and stay up late all the time, until he descended gently into the netherworld of this city of masks and discovered a real world of fantasy, filled with the faces of women and varieties of alcohol, local and imported. As for his great dreams, he locked them up in an "on hold" room inside his head.

They would meet in a big room every day till the end of the night, in an apartment in Khazzan Street, a room that heard an amazing number of unforgettable stories.

Anxious to sleep after a day full of sins, he said, "I feel like something on hold." Then he fell asleep.

He slept a whole day and frightened his family. He choked on his saliva, woke up in a panic, drank a glass of water, and went back to sleep, full of the room's smell, which clung to the pillow. In his head he heard faint groaning noises and a mysterious humming that made his head spin and hurt him till he was close to tears, or close to death, with a slight loss of memory.

When he visited these new dark, low places, he would ask himself what had brought him there, but the next evening he would forget his questions and go back to the same places to smoke dark cigarettes that numbed his head and made him dizzy. He would laugh his head off and listen to the others talking about politics or the results of football matches (which he loved but no longer watched the way he had when he was a student).

Every Thursday he and his family would go to visit relatives, have lunch, and come back in the evening. Many times he didn't go with them but stayed in bed till the afternoon and his father would wake him up when he came back: "Up you get, you enemy of God!" This would signal the beginning of a long fight, which would end with him escaping the house for a while.

After they moved to the new villa, the tradition of having lunch with relatives every Thursday came to an end, and his relationship with his father became like the climate of Riyadh: completely unstable. Sometimes it would be wonderful because of concessions by both sides, and sometimes it would hit rock bottom, while his conciliatory mother took a neutral position on everything that happened. But with his sister Afaf he retained a pure, close, and tender relationship of mutual love. He was her obedient servant, although he was older, so she continued to see him as the perfect young man, whatever he did, and he saw her as the perfect young woman.

The days are all much the same, bringing nothing new, and the truth is always elusive.

Destructive fear of everything.

Fear that begets mistrust of everything.

When he meets them, he blushes at their inquisitive comments.

Their eyes are severe.

They laugh without spontaneity, the kind of laughter meant to offend.

When he frets and when he sleeps, he chokes on his saliva again.

Or he sleeps full of apprehensions, full of demons and intrusive voices that jangle in his head, that spoil and interrupt his slumber.

Is this the dream future I was waiting for? He adjusts his head on the hot pillow. *I want to stay like this so that I can go to her in my dreams, visit her where she sits dreaming, and write about our dreams together, our madness together, our death together—a communal death.*

Now he's thinking about his body, and about his soul, which almost abandoned his body one night, before he drank the glass of water:

Where was my soul before my body existed? There in the sky.

Does the glass of water stop my soul escaping?

Then he entered a state of delirium, reliving what he had experienced and felt, wavering between reality and what he always imagined to be reality, in waking dreams and troubled dreams at night. And there was always the problem of the soul and the body, the symbol of the angst he tried to read in people's eyes so that he could relax a little.

The Silence of Things

IN THE MORNING Khaled ate a cheese triangle with a piece of bread and drank his cup of tea standing up. Then he went out. He was thinking of many things, while behind him many things were falling apart. He thought about the questions the psychiatrist had asked on his first visit and what he would ask in the next session. On the way to work he was distracted. All he could see was the black snake of asphalt stretching in front of him until he reached the office and signed the register late. Then he headed to the clinic, his conversation with his friend the previous week still ringing in his ears.

His friend had said, "That psychiatrist has a bad reputation."

"How so?"

"He harassed some of the nurses and there were problems."

"Perhaps this psychiatrist needs a psychiatrist."

He remembered the previous psychiatrist's questions: "What do you drink? Do you masturbate? Do you love God? Do you love your parents? Do you like people? Do you like life? How are your relationships with women? Do you love your country? How many hours a day do you sleep? Do you smoke? Do you pray regularly?"

He asked the psychiatrist, "What does prayer have to do with it?"

"You just answer and I'll tell you who you are," the psychiatrist said, and laughed.

In the waiting room there were many old newspapers. He picked one up and read the same old headlines about America and Israel and the Arab summit and demonstrations in Cairo against Israel and America. When he heard his name called, he threw the newspaper down and went in to see the psychiatrist. He was thinking that we in this country live in a sealed box far from the rest of the world. He imagined the box floating in a vast ocean, buffeted by waves, without a compass to guide it.

The psychiatrist was firing questions at him, as if he had memorized them, and most of the time the psychiatrist answered his own questions. As soon as Khaled uttered a word, the psychiatrist interrupted, picked up on the word and commented on it with a long spiel.

"I choke on my saliva when I'm asleep," he told the psychiatrist. "And sometimes I lose my memory."

Like a tape recorder, the psychiatrist intoned, "The memory has streets like the city streets you've gone down in real life. These streets have parallels in your head, and in the end they are just streets in your memory but sometimes they resemble dead ends." Enthusiastically, he added: "Try to retrieve the memory when that happens to you. Try to count from one to ten, and your memory will soon recover. This means your condition is normal, but don't give in and don't be weak. Try to register everything that's happened in your life in the form of bullet points, to activate your memory."

Then the psychiatrist called in the next patient.

He left the clinic frustrated, and resolved never to visit doctors again.

The journey between the clinic and home was new and unfamiliar, as if Riyadh had changed into something else, something like the sterile concrete house that they had recently moved into and that they called a villa. Sometimes he wanted to reach out to the villa's malicious spirit and say to it: "I'm not me, and you're not you." Abroad, the world was in ferment, but there were deep spaces of silence in this city. A strident silence that gives you a chance to listen to the city's heart and hear its thoughts. The days were much the same in this city, which did not know if it was pious or decadent—a city that muffled sounds, like a pressure cooker about to explode.

He felt a deep sense of alienation and an urge to cry, while Riyadh whirled him round, from Olaya Street to Mecca Street to Khazzan Street, past the neighborhoods of his childhood, as far as Shumaisi Street and then to the new district of al-Badia, where a few months ago his family's dreams had taken shape in the form of a large but lonely house. The trip from the clinic to home felt like a lifetime. As he turned into his street, he passed a car that was playing loud music. In it, a woman fully clothed in black was sitting next to a man who was smoking and laughing as though dancing, while she nodded along— or perhaps she was laughing too. To the right stood a shop selling the Islamic cassettes that had proliferated in every street, followed by a line of restaurants, tailors' shops, and endless grocery shops, then the recently built central market, which had become a place where lovers met. His car stopped in front of the door of their house. He got out and found his father sitting on the doorstep of the villa.

His father asked him straight out, "Where have you been?"

"At work," Khaled replied.

"I want you to help me with something," his father said.

"Now?"

"Later this afternoon."

He went into the house the family had dreamed of for thirty years, which had now become a tangible reality, but without a soul. Going into the bathroom, he put his head under the tap, hoping to take the edge off the fierce summer heat. He was wondering about the malaise that had struck the whole family since they first set foot in this new neighborhood and moved into this oppressive concrete house a few months earlier; since they left the mud house, the smell of which still clung to his body.

Khaled had thought that their lives would take off to new horizons, but there was no obvious reason for this intense sense of boredom, alienation, and emptiness. Was it because their relatives had now moved out to separate neighborhoods, whereas once they had all lived close to each other? Or was it because his family members were now living apart inside this large desolate house, with separate rooms and private lives of their own? He did not know. He turned the tap off and put a towel on his head. Soft music came from one of the rooms, perhaps his sister's. He came out of the bathroom and went into his room. He decided not to go down for lunch and not to take his clothes off. Going straight to his bed, he threw himself down and turned the cassette player on, which was unlike him. That day he chose to lie on his back, relishing the sensation of his muscles letting go. He was staring at the ceiling as if seeing it for the first time, and when he looked at the floor he felt so dizzy that, unusually, he suddenly fell asleep. Did he need such a change in order to fall asleep so fast? He woke up in midafternoon after an hour of restless sleep during which he dreamed that the new house was full of water up to the ceiling and they were swimming around inside it, like sad fish.

He went down the stairs in four quick bounds, into the darkness of the ground floor. He walked past his mother, who was asleep in the sitting room with a small radio on beside her, tuned to the Quran program broadcasting a reading of the Yusuf chapter. He went through the little garden leading to the street and found his father waiting for him in the street, having just finished the afternoon prayer. They got into Khaled's car together.

"Where to?" asked the son.

"To our old house," said his father.

He set off toward it, wondering whether his father also felt homesick in their new neighborhood and in the vast house for which they had waited so long. He felt a transitory sadness as he thought about the state they were in, fragile as a candle about to go out, a candle fighting to survive against winds blowing from every quarter. He felt that time was like a powerful river that wanted to sweep them all away to places and faces they did not know. He said to himself, "It's boom time, the age of the rich, the powerful, and the wellborn, not the age of the poor, the sick, and the dreamers. It's a time of transition toward a mysterious world we know nothing about." He felt like a lost and useless creature. In the car his father was silent. Khaled wanted to kiss his left hand, which was lying between them on the box that held cassettes, but his father's constant severity held him back.

Why don't I tell him I'm ill? he thought. *Will he be interested? Behind his severity he may be hiding a child whose secrets he will not reveal.*

They reached their old neighborhood. The narrow streets were quiet and slightly dank that sad afternoon. The walls still bore the old graffiti, and the dust preserved the same old footprints. He stopped the car in the street, right in front of the door. His father got out and Khaled got out after him. He opened the door and they went in. Two sparrows escaped through the large hole in the ceiling. His father stopped in the middle of the courtyard, then looked around as though searching for something amid the heaps of dust.

"What are you going to do?" asked the son.

"This way," said his father. "We'll dig here, under these mud walls, then we'll lay strong stones to protect the house."

His father shambled around inside the little house in silence, then asked Khaled to fetch the pick and shovel from the small room. Khaled brought them, and his father began to dig under the crumbling mud wall in the middle of the house, while Khaled removed the soil from the hole.

His father dug so much that he grew tired. He stopped, took a handful of the soil, and smelled it. "What is it?" asked Khaled.

"This damp comes from the septic tank," said his father.

"Should we have the tank emptied?" Khaled asked.

His father didn't answer, just went back to digging.

"Shall I take over?" asked Khaled.

"You don't know how. You mustn't upset the balance of the house."

The father kept digging till he grew tired again, and sat on the mound of earth.

"I'll rest a while," he said.

"That's enough for today. We can bring a workman tomorrow," said Khaled.

"No," he said, and lay on his back.

After a while Khaled noticed that his father had fallen asleep on the soil, just as the sunset call to prayer was about to start. It was beginning to grow dark. Khaled felt pains in parts of his body, and he was shivering like a flickering light. A slight spasm came and went in his head. He leaned back against the wall, feeling as though a bloodstained hand was groping inside his chest, trying to grab his heart. He broke into a cold sweat. He sat on the ground and had a sudden desire to light a cigarette, but he didn't out of respect for—or fear of—the old man sleeping in front of him. His father was now sleeping peacefully and in comfort, while Khaled felt halfway between a mud house in which he had lost interest and a new house for which he harbored no affection.

He watched his father sleeping and remembered how, a few months before they moved to the new district, his father had faced an impossible dilemma when two young men proposed to marry his sister Afaf. One was bearded, with a short thobe, and without a university education. He spoke like a member of the religious police. The other was a graduate, but he smoked. Both were from good families, as they say. He and his mother took the side of the second young man, along with his sister, the party most concerned. But his father and his younger brother favored the first young man. So there were many weeks of consultations and disagreements, until finally his father turned both suitors down.

He looked at the question from another angle.

His view was that this society, which was now moving from one stage to another, from neighborhoods with mud houses to suburbs with new concrete houses, was divided into two camps—a puritanical camp and a camp that was rushing into a new consumer lifestyle at full tilt, and in the middle stood a third camp of people who were lost and adrift, unaware of what was happening around them. Everyone was trying to drag the middle group into their camp, by fair means or foul, and if necessary by brainwashing them. He could see that Afaf was in that wretched third camp, battered by clashing waves, swimming like a sad fish.

So they moved their lives, their ideas, their dreams, their habits, and their fears to new houses. Just inside the new houses they even made separate sitting rooms for men and for women, with separate doors, inside compounds with high walls!

He had heard about strange tumors appearing in society, about horrible crimes committed by adolescents and sometimes by the police themselves—moral decadence, pathological religiosity, corruption, chaos, mugging, prostitution, drugs, robberies. Land prices had soared and a young man could no longer dream of buying a piece of land to build his own house. There were stories one could never have dreamed up—about youngsters who beat an old man to death, about clerics who climbed over high garden walls on behalf of the religious police, about young men who married Thai women and never came back, about young men who died in Afghanistan in the name of jihad, about summer camps to teach adolescents to be religious extremists, to hate life and hate other people. Society had split into two camps, one camp adopting the slogan that God is strict in punishment, the other insisting that God is forgiving and merciful, and everything naturally ended with the words "God Almighty has spoken truly." Meanwhile, in the background, the media were trumpeting that everything was just as it should be.

His father woke up, stood up tall and lean, and brushed the dust off his clothes. He asked Khaled what time it was.

"It's sunset," he said.

"The house needs lots of work. We'll bring the workmen next week," he said.

"Inshallah," said his son.

They left the house and locked the door. Before they got into the car, Sheikh Ibrahim greeted them. He was the local mayor, the imam and caretaker of the mosque, and the real estate agent. He was married, with two wives, and sons and daughters who had all married. He had been quick to buy up the mud houses cheaply from the owners who had fled to the new world in the new suburbs, and he rented them out to poor families and recovered his investment from ten years' rent.

He welcomed them and asked how the house was and whether they planned to sell it.

"We want to fix it up and rent it," said his father.

"Give me the keys and I'll fix it up with the rent money," said the estate agent.

The father agreed immediately and wished him good luck with the house.

"Don't worry, your house is in good hands," said Sheikh Ibrahim.

They went to Sheikh Ibrahim's office next to their house. His father performed the sunset prayer, then discussed the details of the lease with Sheikh Ibrahim, while Khaled sat on a chair by the door watching the silent activity in their little street and thinking of the past, the only remnants of which were memories like passing clouds. He tried to fill in the many dark corners of that time and those places, but so much time had passed that he could shed no light on the events. Everything around was obscure, wrapped in deep expanses of silence, because the street had lost its men and children, along with the women in their black gowns with their raucous laughter.

In this street they had grown up, learned to walk and to talk, to be afraid, to dream, and to be silent too. In the wide street behind him there was a little market that sold everything to everyone, even folk tales and legends, along with various types of gum and powders for those who were sick and for women who had just given birth.

His association with this life, and with the streets of this neighborhood, had a cruel and frightening beginning.

One day, as the street was saying farewell to the last rays of the setting sun, they were playing barefoot in the lane and spying on the people who lived in the mud houses with their wooden doors ajar. They weren't far from the local landmark, a large hole that had been part of their lives since they were born. Suddenly they heard a muffled scream, and Khaled saw a small boy falling into the hole, which looked like an old well. It was a grim moment, alarming to a child. The small boy gave a shriek, maybe with his last breath. Everything was terrifying. There was a large crowd coming home from the city market. People stopped and began to peer into the dark hole that had swallowed the child, while Khaled watched the scene from a distance in horror, like someone who has been electrocuted, shaking and sweating, unable to believe what he was seeing—a human being falling into eternal darkness and swallowed up whole! As the days passed he tried to forget what had happened, but in vain. Homework and playing helped to distract him but many things brought the image back to his mind, and he sometimes had a strange feeling that it was he who had fallen down the hole. At other times he behaved on that basis, as though he were the boy that had fallen. In one dream he saw the hole growing wider and wider and, as it grew, devouring more people, until it swallowed up the whole lane. But when he was half-awake, he found he had grown up and they had moved to a new neighborhood and had new neighbors who owned fancy colored cars and wore brilliant white clothes—neighbors who put perfume on their clothes and drove off through the city streets. As he grew older, he discovered that they were all driving in the wrong direction.

Sitting on the chair, listening without interest to the conversation between his father, the real estate sheikh, and some other neighbors, he suddenly felt like sleeping. They were talking rapidly and cheerfully, as if each of them had found what he sought in the other. There was his austere father laughing with Sheikh Ibrahim. He had never seen him laugh so heartily. He was drinking bitter coffee and eating dates despite his diabetes, and laughing.

Wow, his face does look handsome when he laughs. Why does he hide this handsome face from us, this father who always used to greet my childish presence at the wooden door of the house with such disdain? When I wanted to come in, he would raise his voice, look at me with contempt, and say, "Where have you been, you Jew?"

In his waking sleep in Sheikh Ibrahim's office, he imagined he was being chased by many fathers, all with identical faces and thick beards, each of them wanting to be a father to him, as many fathers as there were streets in Riyadh, chasing him at that very moment, wanting him to belong to them, as though he were a piece of real estate. So many fathers, while he, the sick post-adolescent dreamer, wanted to elude them all and make a fresh start, without certainty and without resolve. And those childish questions about death, God, sex, women, body, and soul—he wanted to get them out of the dark room inside his head, but they melted away inside the room and no longer existed. The questions were overwhelmed by other questions about right and wrong, work, politics, America, and Israel. The new questions killed them off and took their place.

He went back to observing the conversation between the neighbors.

His father and Sheikh Ibrahim, carried away by the pleasure of talking, were pronouncing the letter *k* as *ts*, like all the people of Najd—*keef al-hal* (how are you?), for instance, came out as *tseef al-hal*—but he didn't know how to talk that way. They were talking rapidly and laughing, while he was about to fall asleep. He opened his eyes when they spoke loudly and caught sight of Sheikh Ibrahim looking back at him. He smiled and returned to dozing. He had thought that his was the only family that was tired, detached, dysfunctional, and alienated, but then he started to see ominous signs on the faces of the people he met on his way to work every morning.

He saw the same signs in the face of Sheikh Ibrahim, who was complaining how his children neglected him and how he had no contact with his married daughters. Sometimes the mayor raised his voice, cursing his sons and daughters, cursing the world, and his father would say, "Please don't curse."

He was still thinking about this new transition in their lives, about what it had done to them and what it had done to everyone. Sheikh Ibrahim had built an apartment block and three villas for his children. His father had built them a large villa after selling everything, and it was the same with all the people who were now cursing everything and who didn't know what had happened to make them always so agitated and tense.

After a lengthy conversation, Sheikh Ibrahim, the real estate man, bade them farewell. They left his office and got in the car.

His father was silent almost all the way home, but just before they arrived, without turning his head, he asked, "Why have you rented an apartment?"

"It's closer to work . . ." Khaled started to say.

His father raised his hand to tell him to stop speaking, but remained pensive until they arrived. He got out of the car and Khaled went off to his apartment.

Life on Hold

ALL HIS FRIENDS LEFT after midnight except for Walid, who stayed in the sitting room reading the newspapers. Khaled went into the bedroom, closed the curtains, and turned the air conditioning on. He lay on his back, nauseous after only two glasses, and feeling pain all over his drugged body.

He said to himself, *I'm not going to die. No one dies before his time, before destiny calls. And before death there comes a pervasive smell. That's how some people know their time is drawing near, several days before the end. I don't feel my time is approaching now, even if I can hardly breathe and my head is wracked with pains from late nights and anxiety. Sleep seems a long way off despite my tiredness. Perhaps in two or three days I'll be back to my normal state, but sometimes I feel this circle that surrounds me is firmly closed. You return to your normal life from the world of late nights, you eat, drink and sleep, go to work, visit family and relatives like an upright person, the daily routine, but soon you tire of that and go back again to the world of late nights, friends, and anxiety.*

Something drew him toward that world. Was it the desire to escape from reality, or was it that he was too weak to face a reality he still did not understand?

Every time his father met him, he would ask, "Why are your eyes red?" or "How long is it since you had some sleep, smart ass?"

I feel like something on hold, or a creature that's been tamed.

But now I am free, in this small place that contains all the dreams I have on hold.

He stared at his fingernails all the time, so as not to forget the painful memories: the broken dreams and the old rebuffs. Then he came to his senses and, resentful and disheartened, noticed that he was looking at the soft fingernails of a grown child, a child still full of questions and curses. He remembered his mother's tears and his domineering father out and about in the streets and the child that survived inside him. He could still see himself clearly, running through the streets and lanes, writing the names of his friends on the walls, building houses out of mud, racing through the city, staying up late at night, smoking and drinking, basking in the smell of good times, with dancing and women.

The future might be what he was already going through, what he had been waiting for and what he would continue to await. It might be here now, facing him down like a man, like a pillar of fire, and here he was still without a family or a house of his own. Behold the future! He almost felt he could touch it as it swept like a breeze around the place where he lay in pain. Not only did he feel out of place in his father's house; in this city, for no good reason, he felt he was inferior to everyone else.

Sometimes he felt that what he was going through was nothing but a long dream and he should not trouble himself with the details because it was just a dream, with no basis in reality. But then, with a sudden pang of conscience, he felt with intense certainty that he was living in a reality that was solid and extremely tough. Then the angst and the memory loss recurred. He thought of his mother, his brother, and his sister, and sometimes he felt he was wrong to leave their house, even if he had no desire to go back.

The last time he had met Afaf at his father's house, she told him their brother Ahmad no longer watched television and turned it off whenever he saw her and her mother watching it. He had torn up all the pictures she had drawn and hung in the living room, hidden the tape player, and started to stay out much of the time.

Oh God, how can I sleep when I have this flood of thoughts about things that make me choke? What should I think about so that I can go to sleep?

From the room where Walid was sitting, the voice of the newsreader came to Khaled from the television as, half-drugged, he remembered old times with Walid, remembered the roof of their new house, their drinking parties, and their friends. They would sleep on the roof till the sun woke them. His father was building their new house close to Walid's father's house when Khaled decided to run away from everything to this secluded apartment, far from that watchful world full of people with stealthy eyes who, as soon as they saw you, would launch into sermons. One of them accosted him one evening as he was walking from his father's house to Walid's house.

"Peace be upon you, and the compassion and blessings of God," said the man.

"Peace be upon you," Khaled replied.

The man laughed and tried to put his hand on Khaled's shoulder. Khaled recoiled a little.

"Yes, sheikh, all's well I hope?"

"We and you are the new residents of this blessed neighborhood of ours," said the sheikh. "We want to hold a daily meeting in the mosque."

"Why's that?" Khaled asked.

"To discuss matters religious and worldly."

"Leave our work and our lives to discuss matters religious and worldly?" Khaled said.

The young sheikh laughed and said, "Aren't you looking for something that will count among your good deeds on the Day of Judgment?"

"Working is a form of worship, and sleeping is worship too," he said.

"Not in every case, my son," said the sheikh.

Suddenly a young man appeared. He was no more than twenty years old, and had a beard and a short thobe like the sheikh. He was carrying a bag of cassette tapes. Certain they were training their sights on him, Khaled repeated, "Peace be upon you," and left them puzzled.

I had to leave, he said to himself, laughing in mockery, *because he wanted me to listen to him, then to follow him, then attend his lectures, then distribute his cassettes, and in the end he would have booked me a one-way ticket to Afghanistan, while he would have stayed comfortably here at home with his wives.*

Perhaps many things are as they should be, now.

The pains began to ease, and he began to feel that he existed.

But there was still the memory loss and the doctor's medicine that hadn't worked so far, as well as something he had noticed recently—that he had started talking to himself. Whenever he noticed this strange behavior, he stopped talking. He often felt, when he heard a conversation between two people at work or in the street, that he had heard the conversation before. Then he would suddenly realize that his intuition was mistaken, because there was nothing in front of him but faces he didn't recognize.

Khaled left the bed, went out to the living room, sat on the sofa, and lit a cigarette. He watched the smoke as it blurred the features of Walid, who was sitting on the piece of matting in front of the television. He asked Walid what was happening with his plan to get married. Walid said, "That plan has finally died."

"How so?" asked Khaled.

"I went to their house yesterday evening. I was in high spirits and dressed up like a bridegroom, but her father took me by surprise with some strange questions. He asked me about the relationship between my mother and my uncle.

"'What about it?' I asked.

"He said, 'They say your mother doesn't speak to your uncle, who's her brother.'

"I said, 'Maybe it's a simple disagreement.'

"He said, 'How come, a simple disagreement? And is your uncle really married to so-and-so?'

"'That's true,' I said.

"He laughed and said, 'And your father's brother? Why did they send him to jail last year?'

"'Is this an interrogation?' I said seriously.

"He laughed too, and said, 'No . . . but I don't want my daughter to live in such circumstances, especially as she wants to finish her university education.'

"Then I realized the reason he was reluctant to approve the marriage was his snobbery about his new job. I made my apologies and left, though I was stunned by the fancy stuff I saw in his house, when he used to be so poor."

Walid continued enthusiastically, "All the walls in his house are covered in glass cabinets full of books and antiques. Can you imagine? How can they read when they spend all their time shopping or in hotels or out on the town, even if they do memorize a few intellectual phrases to make an impression when they speak in public? That house is a testament to the consumer lifestyle that has taken root among us."

Khaled put out his cigarette.

"Forget it, let's change the subject," he said. He asked Walid what was in the newspapers.

Walid replied, "Remember the proverb that goes: 'We went to recover our stolen camels and the rustlers took our sheep and goats as well'? Well, that's what's happened to the Arabs who tried to recover Palestine and lost Iraq. That's why this stupid terrorism was a violent reaction to American and Israeli terrorism and to the way Arab governments have neglected their own peoples for half a century."

Khaled replied in a somber tone, "Two days ago I visited my family at home and the atmosphere was suffocating. My sister told me our brother Ahmad had come into her room and taken the cassette player because it was sinful, as he put it. I went to his room and asked him, 'Why did you do that, Ahmad?' 'It's sinful, brother!' he shouted. I said, 'The machine was in her room and you invaded her personal property.' 'We're in the same boat, and if it sinks we'll all drown,' he said. Imagine, such poetic piety! A boat, drowning and sinful. I told her I'd put a stop to it and get her cassette player back.

"Anyway, I photocopied a page from an Arabic newspaper with an article by an Arab scholar of Islamic matters, entitled 'The Practice of the Prophet Condoned Singing and Associated Arts,' and in the article there were dozens of authoritative traditions that all approved of singing. I put the piece of paper under the door of Ahmad's room, and then I received his answer—that he didn't recognize such traditions. Of course that's his right, but he doesn't have the right to impose his opinion on others when they think he's wrong."

"Don't make too much of it," said Walid. "It's all the rage in the country these days, and Ahmad's going through adolescence anyway. He might grow out of it. But have you noticed? Everything's gone to pieces. People's relationships have gone to pieces, the workplace has gone to pieces, and family relationships have gone to pieces. We're sunk in huge religious, political, and economic contradictions. Real neighborhoods are dead, real society is dead, real people are dead, and we can no longer pull ourselves together again to get out of this giant mess."

Walid stopped for a moment and then continued, "I'm not pessimistic, my friend, but everything points in that direction, because from a distance it's a bleak picture, and society's ills and now this puritanism have been the work of dark forces with an interest in poisoning society. Doesn't Islam itself call for moderation and condemn extremism?"

Walid noticed that his friend had closed his eyes, so he suggested he go to sleep. Khaled, half dazed, said, "When I get into this wretched state, my temperature goes up and I feel dizzy. I black out for a while, as if time had suddenly stopped, as if I'd fainted, and when my memory comes back, it comes back stronger and deeper than before, so much so that I feel that the details of my childhood are taking shape in the space between you and me. I think about my childhood, about who made me the way I am, questions about existence that bring my body to the verge of separating from my soul, and I sink into a powerful, lucid dream that makes me feel like someone adrift, someone trapped in a fitful sleep. I feel my soul flying off, abandoning my mind, and everything collapses around me as if I'm in some sensational movie scene."

Walid asked him with a laugh about the medicine the doctor had prescribed. Khaled also laughed, and said, "I stopped taking it after he advised me to stimulate my memory by counting from one to ten or by writing."

"And what did you write?"

"I don't want to write when I'm depressed, because then I see life sinking into chaos and despair, with people asking everything but questions that tackle things head on. Everyone hides and suppresses their questions, and then poses the same questions in the form of pathological outbursts, but I've read about a smell that people can detect before it comes out of the pressure cooker, before the earth breaks its silence, as we build another dream, another country halfway between the city and the desert, dreaming that a ship will arrive from the ends of the earth. We see things with blurry eyes, half asleep and half awake. Will the new free writing emerge clearly now? Will it go on its rampage before the ship sinks, before the pebbles catch fire in the nearby mountains, and the flowers ignite in their vases?"

The rays of dawn peeped through the sitting room window. Walid rose from where he had long been sitting, put on his head cloth, and left. Khaled went out of the sitting room and walked around the apartment looking for the sleep he had missed and for a beautiful face that was lost. "My God, I need you, Amira!" he yelled out.

A Hazy Waking State

HE HUNG UP THE PHONE and felt something new coursing through his veins.

On the way to the room he felt saddened.

He stopped and looked at his face in the mirror that stood in the middle of the sitting room. Absurdly, he felt that some stray object was going to break through the wall behind him and lodge in his back.

He shivered and ducked a little. In the wake of that sudden feeling, he realized he had suppressed a laugh at what was happening outside, but he continued to enjoy the idea of that stray object that was going to impale him from behind.

His face had new features that he hadn't seen in a long time. In his new guise he looked older, or more anxious, or perhaps both, with a new fear that betrayed a new spirit, but the pangs of conscience—the fear, the doubt, and the choking on his saliva—were still there.

I don't want to sleep now, after two glasses that I didn't enjoy and a repetitive, boring conversation, he said to himself.

He put the kettle on the stove and stayed nearby to watch the steam rising and to look at the small window. Through the shutters he could hear the jumbled sounds of neighbors—men, women, and children talking to each other or talking to their relatives on the phone with soft, musical voices.

He went back to the sitting room with a cup of tea, feeling dizzy, but also with a pleasant and exciting sense of fear. Through the big window came the smell of the air, moist and mixed with a smell of explosives or gunpowder—or was it oil, or charcoal?

For the first time in a long time, he had a feeling that was simultaneously mysterious, pleasant, and frightening. He hadn't felt any of that since childhood, this excitement that intensified all sensations. For many years his senses had been dulled, his view of things was apathetic, and the infrequent events that took place around him were unimportant and unexciting. But here he was, suddenly aware of his existence, and troubled about it, as though expecting the pressure cooker that had long been boiling to suddenly explode and reveal the truth.

The cup of tea had a different taste and smell. "Everything is different now," he said, "even the behavior of many people, who are now more excitable and more selfish. Does fear do all that?"

As he tried to fall asleep, he imagined walking down many streets, meeting many faces and speaking to many people. The people were sitting on the stoops of their houses staring at the sky.

As he tried to fall asleep he grew more anxious, sad, and frightened.

Sleep didn't come, but his body was tired and in pain, as if pricked with needles. At that moment he felt he was living in a new state, sunk in a strange stupor, not between sleeping and waking but possibly between a faint reality and a dream that had greater impact than reality and that he felt was the true reality. He went back in his memory. His thoughts revolved around images, then quickly jumped closer to the present in an attempt to bring together the dispersed images. He thought about his father and mother, his forlorn sister, and his brother Ahmad, who was about to fade out of their lives. He thought about many things that were happening, the meaning of which he did not know, because for years he had yearned for something new, something that would change their lives and their ideas, so they could make a fresh start after years of living in a closed box. But everything had collapsed abruptly, and life went on calmly and in deathlike tedium.

He closed his eyes in a moment of rare pleasure, but at that crucial moment he heard the doorbell ring.

He opened the door, but no one was there. For a while he looked at the calm, dark doorway, then went inside and shut the door, with a sense that someone was coming in with him, a man from former times, bearing a history he had to find out about. He told the imaginary visitor, "I have something to confess, my friend. I'm not as busy as I had you believe for many years. I've been staying at home without going out for several years. I rarely go out, and this isolation has taught me how tranquillity can be a noble man, or a virtuous woman, or a painting that is transparent, precious, and admired. It has taught me how to put a high wall between myself and the voices that are loudest, that are most offensive and most miserable. My mind is full of many things: streets and lanes, faces, questions, and conversations, houses and markets. It's full of women, men, and children, things that wait for me when I go out, and to which I return breathlessly, to find them placed carefully on the table in anticipation of my arrival, and only then do I remember where I put my head before I went out. I set aside some special time and conjure up the ecstatic poet and the artist who hears voices, to receive them all."

He went back to the room, the echo of the doorbell ringing in his ears. Suddenly he felt exhausted. He stopped, leaned against the nearby wall, walked on a little until he reached the bedroom, and threw himself down on the bed. For several minutes he lay monitoring his rapid heartbeat until he gradually began to feel that he did exist, but his memory was faint. For a fleeting moment, he felt homesick in this room, then blacked out for a moment. When he came round, for a moment he didn't know where he was in the house.

Am I in the sitting room? he wondered.

The darkness didn't give him a chance to move or to see.

I was in the room before the lights suddenly went out like that (did they really go out?), or at any rate, before I felt the great darkness around me. Yes, in the room, but the room seems too small. It may be the reception room next to the sitting room.

He reached out his hand, followed it with his body, and stumbled into the dark, eerie void. He stood, raised his hand, approached the wall, leaned his back on it, and observed the gloomy scene.

A pain in his eye reached his brain: *Where are my glasses?*

All I know is that I was relaxing on the bed when I woke up frightened to raucous voices—the voices of men, women, and children, as if they were at some party. It was a troubled sleep, and I was somewhere between a hazy waking state and an ambiguous slumber. I recall some images and am trying to focus my mind to find out if they are real images or just dreams—images that are very close by but rapidly retreat into the distance when my brain is tired.

So perhaps the door was open and they came in.

I think I saw them coming in, but they were busy, they were talking to each other in loud voices. I saw them like ghosts coming and going, entering the rooms, the bathrooms and the kitchen, and coming out, talking loudly.

I focus on the very end of the sitting room in the distance (I've started to be certain that that's where I am). With difficulty I can make out the bright blue curtain on the window that opens onto the passageway, the only thing shining in this darkness except for a faint light coming through the half-open door.

Did I run toward this light a short while ago? My eyes still hurt and I still can't find my glasses.

I remember that I reached home after a long excursion. I changed my clothes and threw myself exhausted on this bed. Where's Walid? I was just relaxing with my eyes open, my body tired, absentmindedly, in a strange state somewhere between waking and sleeping, when I suddenly noticed the pitch dark, the strange images, and the many faces and things I'm trying to recall, then those voices, and the people speaking, who circled around me making such a din. There's a pain that sometimes reaches my head, and there's no distinguishing between reality and imagination. I told myself that this state of mind had nothing to do with my glasses, but where are they? The truth is clear to me now. They came into the house while I wasn't looking, perhaps when I had a short blackout. Has night fallen?

I'll be certain I exist when I cross this dark space in front of me, when I go into the kitchen, when I pick up a glass full of cold water and pour it down my throat in one gulp to quench this old thirst. I'm going to cross this sitting room in spite of these bodies coming and going, and their voices that have invaded my quiet space, and when I've quenched my thirst, I'll go back to the long sofa to watch the rest of the drama unfold in this new sitting room, so that I can write about this mysterious haze between sleep and waking.

But suddenly I find I'm descending to that zone where I might be able to relax a little or submit to something like clinical death, which makes you end your life looking earnest.

I go down there, timidly. I turn off the house lights and go down to her territory, safe and submissive, to the land of the beloved I have lost. I go down looking for her, looking for a vision of her, forgiving myself for my minor sins and telling myself to merge with everything that was there, in the hope of catching the vision, running away from life, escaping from small wars and struggles here and there that throw their sparks onto my broken life, escaping from absurdity, from always running around senselessly. I go down calmly.

And when I've settled at a lower level, I see narrow, dark paths. I see her radiant face, and she invites me to sit on a dreamy couch.

My spirit stirs, and my heart begins to stir too, or rejoice or dance.

I begin to sense the child that I was, when my new spirit took me back to new places.

"A new spirit will arise within you," she says, "and you will overflow with poetry and song and dance, to shake off the dust of years that was clinging to your old spirit."

I close my eyes at this new level, and see myself from afar, dancing and singing until evening comes and darkness descends and life is still.

She says, "Go back to your family, son of life, for now you are a new man."

I come back up to this level and see the child I was and the man I still am meeting on a narrow, dark road, and behind them a radiant face luring me, possibly Amira's, and I say, "All women are beautiful."

I remember that I have recently celebrated it—a face that blazed with light like a flower.

"The child inside me has not died," I say.

The old places haven't died, or the new.

My memory hasn't died.

And this is a new dawn rising over me.

And the sun is shining like the face of a happy girl.

And there are new melodies.

My soul is at rest.

There's a mysterious truth, more evident than before, about to express itself.

Outside I see a longing that wants to go there with me, to my new territory, a longing that used to come over me long ago, and I didn't know how to interpret it.

He woke up from this agitated, anxious sleep to the small joy of knowing that he was better now, after a short rest, but some portion of his original sadness began to impose itself; a mythical sadness that reminded him of old faces in old markets he knew, and of the magical ambiance of lanes with a smell that coated the walls of the houses with preposterous colors, and an anxious joy and an old sadness that seemed to be his eternal fate, with a slight sense of elation that put his nerves on alert. He remembered his untamed sexual desires, which he often ignored, and he began another life, in search of an elusive truth.

Another Life

NOW . . . another life.

In the beginning, he only wanted to activate his dormant memory.

He was looking at the blank paper in grave silence.

A beautiful image was now in front of him:

A piece of paper . . . and silence.

A blank, silent piece of paper, on which he counted from one to ten, with no real desire to write, and in front of him there was a blank canvas.

He was thinking about those pieces of paper preserved long ago in the dark chambers of his soul, or his head, or his madness.

Silent pieces of paper, filled with dates, images, dreams, joys, pains, and memories.

Whiteness seeking the secret of meaning.

—∾—

He could write about a boy's life that began in the middle of old Riyadh after the modest economic boom at the start of the 1950s. That life faded, and another life, an adult life, began at the start of the 1970s, when people moved out of the mud-built neighborhoods into suburbs where the houses were built of concrete and steel, with high walls and sealed windows. And when the dream came true, did it live up to the promise of bliss it offered when it was just a dream?

His adolescence, which coincided with the period when their neighborhood was dying out, was a period of sexual awakening for him, and also of political awakening in the Arab world, after Sadat's visit to Israel and the wave of rebellion against many things—and so there were many stories with which he might justifiably reactivate his memory.

He could leave aside those momentous issues that people have written off as history because they weren't interested in them in the first place. He could leave aside Gamal Abdel Nasser, the Arab–Israeli wars, King Faisal's oil boycott of America, the occupation of the Grand Mosque in Mecca by Juhaiman, the peace agreement between President Sadat and Israel, the Lebanese civil war, the Israeli invasion of Lebanon, the Iraqi occupation of Kuwait, then the invasion of the world by modern communication devices, and the American occupation of the Middle East, because who was he to take an interest in these major matters—matters that now seemed laughable?

On this silent whiteness he would try to create a new spirit, parallel to the spirit that had raged malignantly inside him for many years.

A spirit that tried to fathom the meaning of it all.

To write openly . . . about the places he had been, the smell of which he almost felt he could touch, the sweet taste of which lingered on his tongue.

Now . . . another life.

So, at the start of the last century, four farmers from a village in the Riyadh area, driven by hunger, went out looking for a new life, carrying a water bag and a sack of dry dates, which helped them cover twenty leagues across the desert on foot.

In the village they had left, people said they had gone to Kuwait to work at sea, while others said they had gone to work on the well-watered farms of Riyadh. But most of the village men, though they and their families were wasted by hunger, never thought of abandoning their hardscrabble farms and their arid land. They would pray to their Lord every evening, that He might bless them with rain, until they forgot about the men who had left, never to return. They buried their dead when they died of hunger, then repaired to the mosque to pray again.

In the first three days of their march, the four men were enthusiastic and could cover long distances, because many years of labor had given them strength and endurance. They walked long hours, and the dream of a new life in the city of Riyadh raised their spirits as they hurried on by night and by day.

On the evening of the fourth day, they rested under a large tree, had a drink, and ate some of the dry dates, then slept till dawn. They prayed, and walked on until their dates ran out and they had only a little water. They felt they had covered more than half the distance. They rested a little, then resumed their journey, oblivious to the mysterious voices that surrounded them from the deepest darkness of the desert. They walked a long time, with their grand dreams, and in great sorrow at parting with their families and loved ones. Exhausted they rested, their faces lined with fatigue, misery, and anxiety, because they had run out of dates and water, and there were no villages nearby to quench their deep thirst. Words were no longer their primary means of expression: the way they looked at each other and at the pitch-black desert night served as another language, cruel and fearful. Their faces were full of a fear that was almost palpable, like a smell that floated around their broken spirits and their exhausted bodies.

During the night, one of the four gave the other men a strange look. He was lying close by, but he smelled something terrifying, and jumped up and ran off with all his remaining strength. He ran a long way and disappeared into the ancient Najdi desert. This man had had a feeling that his three companions, who were in fact his cousins, were thinking of eating him, and just at the moment when he had this feeling, he exchanged mysterious, fearful looks with them and then took to his heels. They were puzzled how this man could have known what was going on in their minds, even if they had not been really serious about eating him.

Close to death, the man reached a small village, which spelled a new life for him after he had run so far in hunger and in thirst. He collapsed, almost lifeless, by the wall of the only mosque in the village. A villager brought him food and water and asked him to wait till the next morning because there was a caravan going to Riyadh, which was not far off.

In the morning the caravan set off, and it reached Riyadh in two days. The man felt reborn and slept several straight days in the Manfouha district in the south of the city. He then worked on a farm in exchange for board and lodging, and protection. He began to think about the family he had left behind in his village. As for his three companions, he erased them from his memory.

This man was Khaled's grandfather. He later married a Riyadh woman who gave birth to Khaled's father, uncle, and aunt. Khaled's father worked with his grandfather on the same farm for several years until they could afford to move out of old Riyadh to the center of what was then new Riyadh, where they built a mud-brick house. By that time many families were settling in the area because some government departments and schools had opened their doors during the reign of King Saud at the start of the 1950s and later that of King Faisal. It was here that Khaled's father married a relative who had moved to Riyadh from al-Washm, northwest of Riyadh. When the grandfather died, Khaled's father become the family patriarch and worked as a messenger in a government office. The family began to prosper somewhat after years of struggle and hard work. They had moved from house to house in the old parts of Riyadh, but they did not sever their ties with people in the village, visiting them at holidays on the public buses, like those that went to the Hejaz.

At the start of the 1970s, when Khaled was about ten years old, he began to wake up to the life around him, and hear about things that had happened. He became aware of the community in their neighborhood, which was rather unhealthy because it lay in a depression, lower than the neighborhoods nearby.

It was a neighborhood that seemed to have emerged overnight from a pile of dust. He often wondered where it had come from, who had chosen the site in the first place and why God had made it so low, and who Umm Saleem was. She was the woman for whom the neighborhood on higher land nearby was named. They said she had lived in the area many years before—an old woman whose husband had died and left her a fortune from farming. She bought large amounts of land on the cheap, then sold it off in small plots. The spot where their neighborhood lay was like a big depression, directly south of Khazzan Street and east of the higher land of Umm Saleem, from where even the lowest of the houses could see the big hole they called Shumaisi, with its squat mud-brick houses. In the rainy season, the street leading from Umm Saleem to Shumaisi turned into a river that emptied into their low-lying quarter, and when the rain stopped their quarter looked like a large pond. It might have been the lowest district in the world, and it upset the residents to see the people who lived in higher areas enjoy the rainfall, while they themselves were in complete panic. The old people, who believed that it kept raining because God was angry, would shout "God is great!" and "There is no god but God!" and he would wonder why God had these constant outbursts of anger and what sins they had committed to incur His wrath.

The family house lay in the middle of this neighborhood. The people had finished off their houses rather haphazardly, and the streets were no more than fifteen feet wide, some even narrower, and some were dead ends because the ends were blocked by other houses.

It was the residents of this neighborhood who had built the mud-brick houses, with help from relatives and some hired laborers, and in most cases the houses were one-story buildings of no more than fifty square meters, with a large open space in the center, surrounded by the bedrooms and the kitchen, and at the entrance there was the sitting room for men and a small bathroom.

The men who labored to build these houses did not know they were also building the streets where their grandchildren would spend their childhood, landmarks in this dreamy Najdi life of simplicity and poverty. In this neighborhood the streets were more important than the houses. They came to know that later, when boredom at home drove them to escape into the streets, where they could act out their small dreams of rebellion and shake off their inhibitions. The streets were long and narrow, lined with mud-brick houses attached to each other, of about the same height, and the wooden doors were mostly left half-open, so that the voices of the neighbors mingled with the voices of the household as if they were all one happy family.

The homes of his mother's parents, brothers, and sisters surrounded them on all sides, so his grandmother on his mother's side never left their house. She was a strong personality, feared by his father and mother, and at the two big feasts she would fill her pockets with candy to give out to her grandchildren, in the same way that she gave all the households a share of the eggs her chickens laid. She took a firm line with any of her grand-children who tried to avoid school by claiming to be ill. He remembered how he would be reading her some-thing he had learned at school, and she would laugh politely without interest — "Clean boys look elegant," for example, and he didn't know what 'elegant' meant, or "The Arab world is my homeland, from Damascus to

Tetouan," which he would read as "The Arab whirl diss my homeland . . ." When his mother's brother started to bring them Arabic magazines, he cut out pictures of Arab capital cities and kept them in a special folder.

They would sprinkle the roof of the house with water to keep down the dust, and gather there after the sunset prayers. His uncles and aunts and cousins would come and reminisce about growing up in the villages around Riyadh, and sometimes his old uncle would flirt with his wife, right in front of them, and they would be embarrassed. In those days, when they came back hungry from primary school, they would invade the bread bin and eat the bread with dates, drink water from the earthen jar, and go to sleep in the afternoon, then go running through the lanes until the call to the sunset prayers. On Friday mornings people would clean their houses until noon, while the children ran around in the narrow dusty lane. Through the gaps in the half-open wooden doors, which were painted in every color, the faint light of lanterns shone. The streets stank of stagnant water and dampness, but before noon prayers on Friday the men would bathe with water and soap, and then put on perfume to go to the mosque in a festive mood, to be seen and to see each other. The mosques smelled of incense, which gave the walls a pale tinge. The women filled the kitchens with their racket, while the children were naked as usual. The youngsters came and went in their own white thobes, and the girls stood in the doorways with small cassette players, listening to the songs of Talal Maddah, Muhammad Abduh, and Umm Kulthum. You could also see men sitting in front of their doors in groups, drinking tea and smoking, with the women making a din behind them. It was a wonderful time of reverie, full of the smell of damp and Friday mornings. It was as if the narrow streets were shaded and the neighborhood was half asleep, wandering aimlessly like a drunken ship. Sometimes he saw Amira standing there behind the door, almost out of sight. From a distance she looked as tall as a palm tree, towering sublimely over a lane that looked like a lost little girl beneath her.

The people in the neighborhood were fully attuned to one another, in affection but also in envy and jealousy. When goods started to appear from Japan, China, and Europe, every household wanted to be the first to own whatever was new in the market. They discovered televisions, washing machines, and refrigerators. For many years people had spent their evenings on their doorsteps, sharing stories and the neighborhood gossip, bringing good news and bad. Men, women, and children chatted and told each other jokes, sharing gum and candy and small cups of tea. Nearby stood the local store that sold ice cubes, cans of tuna, and tomato paste, and across the street lay the home of Umm Mahmoud, the Palestinian woman who sewed clothes for the women, and Ibrahim's real estate office where the local men gathered.

One night, when the dawn prayers were called and they were sleeping on the roof of the house, he heard a woman's voice whispering softly, "Get up," like the faint echo of the muezzin's voice in his ear. Her voice reminded him of how, on mornings in the old times, when the voice and the echo were gone, he would feel a cold hand patting his head with the message: "People have to see you in the mosque so that they know you've grown up."

In the damp street, which was bitterly cold, he started to smell unpleasant odors, like the urine of cats or dogs—strong penetrating odors, almost palpable. He put his hands in the pockets of his thobe and veered off down the small, dimly lit street that led to the main street, examining the tiny footprints the children had left in the dust when they were running around the previous evening, kicking stones at the pale street lamps. He was walking along, exploring feelings that were naked as a newborn child—vague feelings much of the time—trying to put all the things he didn't understand back in a familiar framework, so he could enjoy an illusory moment of happiness, but the smell of cat and dog urine filled the lane, staining the walls of the houses preposterous colors and spilling out into the local square to set it ablaze. He thought back to the house that was in danger of falling down, his father and mother, his brother and sister, and the neighborhood: bleak memories that left inside him a trace of mud and dark forests. He walked down the cold lane until prayers were over, then went back home subdued, eager to throw himself back into the warmth of his bed.

One bleak afternoon, the clouds were lower than usual, black, sullen, and alarming. In the middle of the afternoon, heavy rain began to fall. The neighbors came out into the narrow streets and dug channels down the middle to ensure the furious torrents of water kept away from the doors of their low-lying houses and joined up with the water from other streets, but no one knew where this raging tide would go after that. He imagined the water asking "Which way?" as it cascaded into the main street.

In fact, there was no way for it to go, and in the end it would be trapped in the middle of the streets, because the owners of all the houses had reinforced their doorsteps with mud or stone, so the streets were flooded with stagnant water.

On that angry, unforgettable afternoon when the skies broke, after the lightning flashed and the thunder roared, people poured out of their houses because the wooden roofs had split open and threatened to collapse. Everyone fled to the nearby mosque and huddled in the courtyard, which was roofed with palm fronds, while the men lifted up their thobes and started to carry out their usual tasks. They went up on the roofs to fill the gaps with cement, because none of them wanted to see their ancestral homes fall down before their eyes and they knew they had no future without these houses, which might collapse at any time. At that moment, he remembered when he had helped his father build their house.

At times like these you remember the past and worry fearfully about the future, and humanity seems like a feather in the wind.

In the mosque Khaled's mother rested on a pile of blankets they had brought from home and leaned back against a mud pillar with a stone base. Around her lay many of the local women and children, half asleep and half afraid.

He saw a woman who lived nearby come up to his mother and whisper, "Does your house have stone foundations?"

"No," said his mother.

"I heard the house next to the bakery collapsed on top of the people living there at noon today," said the woman.

"May they rest in peace," said his mother.

Then the neighbor came closer and, at his mother's side, he could hear the woman's heavy breathing. "Did you hear the BBC this morning?" she asked.

"No," replied his mother.

"They've caught a group of criminals and they're going to kill them in al-Safa on Friday," she said.

"What did they do?" his mother asked.

"They wanted to turn the country into a republic," said the neighbor.

"A republic?"

"Yes. I mean a country without a government. I mean anarchy."

"Thank God for exposing them and foiling their evil schemes," said his mother.

His mother knew that the woman was taking lessons from a woman who taught the Quran. It was also this neighbor who had taught Khaled's mother how to tune in to the BBC to hear world news.

His mother looked up to the sky, which was calmer now, and turned to the neighbor. In a low voice meant to frighten her son, she said, "My son wants a republic in our house—anarchy, that is."

The neighbor, who had big beautiful eyes, was shocked. She put her hand across her mouth.

"Whenever I tell him not to do something, he shouts in my face and says, 'I'm free!'" said Khaled's mother.

The woman turned to the boy, knowing he was the one intended, and their eyes met. Then she quickly turned to his mother and said, "That's kid's talk, my dear."

"We'll have to brand this boy's head," added his mother, and laughed as she looked up at the sky. She began to mutter religious formulas such as "Praise God" and "There is no god but God." Young Khaled was sitting next to the neighbor's daughter and playing with her fingers, which were shaking from fear.

After the rain stopped, they went back home. Half the sky was still overcast, but in the morning all was calm. The colors were clear and the lane smelled of mud.

He refused to go to school, and from the courtyard he watched the sun rising in the sky. The light that fell on their house from the east was fresh and comforting, intimate. At noon when he heard his father come home, he ran off to the little room, and the little window let in a wonderful patch of light that fell in the middle of the room. It came and went as the clouds passed, and he began to doodle on the blank paper in front of him. He was thinking that he didn't just hate school; he sometimes hated home too, in some obscure way.

Umm Amira, their neighbor, came in and told his mother about some houses that had fallen down. Earlier she had pinched his ear and whispered, "You'll go to school tomorrow." He said, "Okay," picked up his crayons, and started to draw a picture of her daughter's pretty face. He was glad his house stood opposite the door to their house so that when their door opened he could see right in. Sometimes the girl would come over, and his mother would ask after her family and after her grandmother, who was memorizing the Quran although she was blind and illiterate. The girl and her young brothers would sweep the street every Friday, then sprinkle it with water until the dust turned red and settled, and did not blow in the wind, so that the streets would have a delicious damp smell. When they had finished this task, they would go inside, have a bath, put on clean clothes, and line up at the front door watching people come and go in the lane.

He remembered how, early one morning, as he was getting ready to go to the local bakery, he saw one of the women next door pick up something he couldn't see clearly from the doorstep of the house next to hers. She ran home when she saw him. He asked his mother about the mysterious incident and she didn't reply, and he had a feeling she was hiding something. Somehow the incident made him think of the world of magic and conjuring, and he drew a picture of the woman next door with a magic lantern next to her, a little girl inside the lantern staring out with piercing eyes. On the other side of the white sheet he drew a beautiful round face looking down on the lane from on high, and on the face he wrote "Amira."

The western horizon still loomed dark and the darkness soon spread and covered the sky over the city. It was darkness at noon, and everyone everywhere looked exuberantly happy, with a touch of fear.

When he was a little older, he began to deal with his family in a different spirit, a new spirit, clear and elated. He would take a cup of tea, flavored with lemon, and go out into the street to examine a new cloud that was about to drop rain on the walls of the houses, or to contemplate the nearby mist. He was sitting on the doorstep one time when a brown-faced stranger came up to him and asked what the area was called.

"New Shumaisi," he said.

"So this is it," he replied. "Do you know so-and-so?"

"No, I don't."

"He's a driver in some government department and he has a house in this lane."

"I don't know him," Khaled repeated.

"He's a good man, and poor. My brother borrowed some money from this man," he added, speaking in a strange way. "Ever since my brother died, I've been looking for this man." Then he stopped speaking and left. It began to rain, and the dust on the ground turned to mud, with tiny runnels of water. The weather was dark, beautiful, and mysterious. It was growing darker, and the rain fell gently in waves. The neighbors began to stick their fearful heads out through the half-open doors of their houses. The man returned and came up to Khaled, as strange as ever, with a green winter thobe and a high collar that reached to his ears and a strange little scarf. When he spoke, you felt he had lost the power of speech, because he was stammering out syllables and broken words that he had trouble pronouncing.

The man was standing in front of him, trying to conceal an obvious smile, and then asked him if they had any old things they didn't need in the house.

"Like what?" asked Khaled.

The man gave an embarrassed laugh and said, "Pots and pans . . . clothes? You know, houses usually have things like that."

"We don't have things like that," said Khaled.

There was a heavy silence, and then the man said, "Do you know somewhere I can work?"

"No."

"I've been released from prison but I can't find work. I'm not a criminal. I borrowed some money and couldn't pay it back, but ..."

"God be with you," said Khaled.

The man took a small notebook out of his leather bag. "Could you write your name in this?" he asked, pointing to the notebook and laughing.

"What is it?" Khaled asked.

"To help the poor," the man said. "You make a contribution and I record your name."

"Who are you?" he asked.

"A philanthropist."

"No, thanks," said Khaled.

The man walked on, playing with the children while he waded down the muddy street as though the mud didn't exist. He looked back at Khaled with frightening eyes.

Fast asleep one dream-filled night, he saw a strange cat crouching near his bed and staring at him with cruel, fiery eyes. In the cat's face, he saw a distorted version of the strange man's face. The cat took a step toward him, crouched as if to pounce, then gave a long, deep, frightening meow. He watched its movements carefully, in case it tried to take him by surprise and pounce at his face. As he watched, the cat let out another slow meow, wailing at him. He saw the sparks flashing from its blue eyes, and he moved back a little, but then the cat let out a long scream, and he woke up. In the morning he wondered where people like the strange man came from.

The image came to him from afar, as clear as the full moon. It was late on a magical afternoon, and the women were hurrying home from their neighbors' homes in their black gowns, across the dust and down the wide streets that led to the back lanes where their houses stood. The children were kicking up the dust with their constant running, and the young men were gathered on street corners, and the older men were on their way back from the local markets that sold goods cheaply. Elsewhere you could hear soft whispers from the doorways of the houses, of girls and young women carefully watching the activity in these little streets and listening to popular songs.

At the end of the small street there was an isolated mud house, a small house with one room opening on to a bathroom and a small courtyard roofed with palm fronds. The Arabic teacher lay on a wooden bed in the middle of the room, which looked out on the street through a low window. He was lying there with the door locked, and the world behind the door was passing strange.

The last rays of the afternoon sun shone into the room through the low window.

Perhaps the teacher was finally asleep.

The teacher closed his cavernous eyes and went to sleep. He started dreaming deeply and forgot his sorrows, entering another time. There perhaps someone happy who loved life would emerge, walking through the streets at leisure, going round the shops and watching people.

There perhaps he would see his life and cheer up, meet his long-lost friends and laugh with them. There perhaps he would run after his old dreams, in the hope that his tired soul would take comfort in them, or that he could put together the fragments of his life that had fallen apart long ago.

His eyes were pinned to the ceiling and his cheeks glowed in the rays of the departing sun. His tall body shivered slightly whenever his eyes blinked. Still groggy from drinking the day before, he pricked up his ears to all the noises coming from outside his little world.

Perhaps he was sleeping now.

Or perhaps he was getting out of bed now, exhausted as usual. He stood by the window, trembling as he wept.

Perhaps he was sleeping now. Perhaps he would sleep forever.

The wife of the Arabic teacher, who had left the school, asked him, "What's happened to you, you men?"

"What?" he asked.

"Men! They're either ill, or tired, or they never leave home," she said.

But he just lay there, feeling the memory of ancient sorrows.

The doctor examined him and gave him an injection, then asked him, "How do you feel now?"

The man shut his eyes and, in a voice that smelled of death, said, "I feel as if I want . . . to sleep," though he knew he had just woken up.

The sheikh from the mosque removed the teacher's clothes and poured saffron water on his body. He went on reciting the Quran until he was exhausted, because the sick man took no interest in anything. All he did as he lay there was look with surprise at the sheikh's face, then turn away and fall asleep. Then a smell of sadness and anger appeared in the lane and started to spread, coating the walls with a strange grayness, and people said many things about life and God's anger. The sheikh had already left the sick man's house, praying for God's protection from the accursed devil.

In another room, permanently lit, at the top of that large mud house, lived the art teacher, a young man who loved his room and had filled it with paintings. He listened to Arab radio stations and drew, and when they visited him, he talked about the Arab world as if he was talking about his own beloved village, with a fear of everything in his eyes. To escape his fear, he took to drawing and writing, and the youngsters in the lane didn't understand anything when they read what he wrote or looked at his drawings. At night they took him with them to the main street and they had dinner together. Then they returned to their homes, or went to the Arabic teacher's house to chat with him, or drink with him, until the early hours, until the Arabic teacher closed his door and retired for the night.

The Taste of Sugar

HE BEGAN HAVING POWERFUL THOUGHTS about sex, starting from a particular moment that was like a spark that set his body on fire. One Friday morning, when he went to the local bakery, he found it full of men and boys and girls waiting in a long line. He stood with them, awaiting his turn, and after ten minutes a girl slightly younger than him pushed into the line and stood between him and her younger brother. She stepped back to make space for her brother and their bodies touched. Her hair brushed his face and he caught a whiff of scented shampoo. He immediately remembered Amira, who would have been the same age and height and had the same trim figure. For him this was an unfamiliar moment full of mystery, excitement, and the promise of love. It made him deeply aware of the life he was now living and of the new blood now coursing through his dry veins as he stood in that highly charged line at the bakery. The only thing to spoil the moment was that one of his school colleagues was right behind him, harassing him and laughing at him. Khaled remembered that the boy had once called him stupid because he was taciturn at school, although Khaled had better grades. The boy would get angry when Khaled called him a street kid. Now the boy was trying to take his place in the line. At first Khaled didn't understand what exactly the boy wanted, and it took him a while to catch on that the boy wanted to be next to the girl. When he realized that, he immediately decided to hit the boy in the face, but at the very moment that he decided to launch his attack, as he turned slowly toward the boy to put his plan into effect, he was taken by surprise by a powerful blow that made his head spin, and he blushed in embarrassment. He ran out of the bakery to catch him, but the boy escaped and went back to his place. He looked at everyone around him in embarrassment, tears welling in his eyes.

On that day, after the incident in the bakery, he began to ask himself many questions about what his reluctance to talk meant. *Why don't I start defending myself before some boy attacks me?* So he decided to slap the boy on the face when he met him on Saturday at school, and he thought about how he might come closer to Amira, in the hope he could smell the scented shampoo in her hair.

For many days he was obsessed with the idea of kissing her, and the idea persisted for months without him carrying it out. He merely felt he had started to take an interest in her and to feel warmer toward her, and he didn't exactly know what all this meant.

Am I content, am I happy in my life?

These were the daily questions he never tired of.

The answers covered piles of paper that he preserved like title deeds. He went back to them whenever he felt anxious or miserable, and convinced himself that everyone experienced these feelings, which hovered halfway between joy and sorrow. And then he began a phase of reading everything.

Amira became his friend. He started to go to her family's house, and she started coming over to his. Early one morning during the summer vacation, he ran to her doorstep as usual and found her there. She had left the main door open and was sitting next to the doorstep. She was playing with the mud she had made by adding water to the dust, drawing brides and bridegrooms in it. He sat down next to her and she told him about the local people, what they did when they were inside their homes and what they talked about. He watched the slender girl, who moved gracefully in front of him, a timid, mischievous look in her eyes. She was wearing a short, torn pink nightshirt and her hair was tied in a plait. She was a year younger than him but was very knowledgeable. She told him about the neighbor who worked for the local council and who hit his wife if the water went out into the street when she was cleaning the house; the woman who read the Quran over people who were sick; the neighbor who had married a young Indian bride; the girl who was possessed by djinn (they said that when she was asleep, her spirit filled the courtyard with a strange smell); and about another neighbor who was expelled from university, grew his hair long, and went off carrying a radio in one hand and a small clothes bag in the other, leaving the neighborhood, the city, and the country. He hadn't been back for years and his mother still wept for him. She told him about many things on moonlit or dark evenings, and on days when all they could see of the sun was a glow that would have cheered the downhearted. When she spoke her arms and legs shook, and then her whole body. She was soft and pretty, with a sympathetic voice. Sometimes they would argue. He would threaten her with his little slingshot, and when she was angry she would pull his hair until he was close to tears, then run away. Once he gave her a cassette player that his mother had bought him after he passed fifth grade. She put the machine on their doorstep and played songs by Talal Maddah and Abadi al-Jawhar at high volume. He happened to look the other way and saw his father coming from the market with a bag of vegetables on his head and a red rooster in his arms. Khaled took the tape recorder and ran off home. His father came in, and behind him Amira, who was amazed by the large bird. His father threw the rooster down in the middle of the courtyard and it ran around in panic, its feathers flying.

His father came up to him and slapped him as usual in the evening, saying, "I'll lock you up if you take the tape player out in the street again." Khaled cried and went looking for the rooster with tears in his eyes. He sensed that Amira pitied him and that made him even more embarrassed. "Come here," he begged her, between sobs. Then, together with his brother and sister, they trapped the rooster in a corner until it submitted, and began to examine it. It was a massive rooster that looked like a peacock, and it looked back at them like a man. His father had strange impulses like that—he would go to market in the afternoon and come home before sunset with some weird creature: a billy goat, a rabbit, some pigeons, and this time a rooster; a rooster that was now trapped in the corner, and the confrontation between them had begun. They stood facing each other, each looking at the other as an adversary, until Amira finally stepped toward it and tried to win it over. The rooster warmed to her and suddenly it settled in her lap and looked up at her face, then with hostility at his face. "Shut your eyes and I'll make the rooster kiss you," she said. He shut his eyes and felt the bird's beak touching his face. He kept his eyes closed until Amira gave her order: "Open your eyes," and he opened them. The rooster was waiting for him; it jumped up from her lap and pecked him in the eye. The girl ran off to her family's house and he cried until nightfall. His mother put salty water in his eye and he went to sleep almost like an invalid, with his younger brother and sister nearby. He woke up in the middle of the night and saw that everyone had gone to bed, so he went to the kitchen, took a piece of flat bread, and filled it with sugar. He went to the small room, turned on the television, and started to eat. The colored plastic mat on the floor had shrunk and the bare floor was visible, revealing a flaky and pitted concrete surface, like the ridges on a piece of sloping ground. As he sat there, he felt the room leaning; he was sitting at an angle and thought the ground was tilting toward the door. He was engrossed in watching the moving pictures coming from the television screen. In his hand he had the piece of bread with sugar, in his other hand a cola, and at his side a book of Arabic texts, to memorize a war song by Antara bin Shaddad. Talal Maddah was singing in full flight when the lights went off as usual, the television screen went dark, and the room descended into pitch blackness. The whole lane was also blanketed in darkness; everything had gone out. He stood up, confused, and started to stumble out of the tilting room, dragging his fear behind him. The courtyard engulfed him and he groped for the mud column that stood in the middle of the yard, then took hold of it. He turned to the left for a moment and saw his mother lying in a corner of the courtyard, which was open to the moonlit sky, with his brother and sister around her. His father was asleep on the roof. He didn't realize that his mother was awake until he heard her ask, "Where are you going?"

"To the street," he answered.

He turned right and walked past the bathroom with a curtain for a door. He breathed in the stifling summer air and reached the door leading directly to the outside. He opened it and a pleasant draft of air hit him. He had heard low voices coming from the neighbors' dark houses, from some of which came the faint light of a candle or a gas lamp. He heard other sounds from the end of the small street, where some of the local youngsters were gathered, chatting and smoking. He sat down on the doorstep, the sugar sandwich in his hand, and felt a pain around the eye where the rooster had pecked him. Then he saw a small stone rolling in the dust in front of him in the midst of the deep calm. He looked up to see where the stone was going, saw that the neighbors' door opposite was ajar, and noticed a slight movement in the darkness within. He stood up and walked across to the neighbors' doorway, stood in front of the dark opening, and started to examine the interior with curiosity. He couldn't see anyone. He leaned his head forward and suddenly a hand appeared from the depths of the darkness, giving him the fright of his life. The hand pulled him inside by his hair. Another hand covered his mouth and a girlish voice gave a hushed, involuntary laugh. He started to breathe rapidly, his heart raced, and his body trembled like a flickering flame. He stood there a few seconds, enjoying the moist softness of the fingers on his mouth. He raised his hand and it met the girl's soft chest. He had an urge to fondle the body in front of him, so he raised his other hand slowly and wrapped his arms around her shoulders, then pulled her soft body to his chest. The two little faces touched gently and he could smell her breath. He remembered the girl at the bakery and everything grew more intense. She was trying to slip away quietly and he was giggling so that she wouldn't detect what he really desired. He moved closer to her, trying to cling to her. She tried to escape but he held her tightly for some moments. He sat her on the bottom step of the inner staircase, lifted her clothes up and kissed all over her naked body for some minutes before the lights came on, interrupting his enjoyment. The courtyard of their house was lit up in front of him and he saw her family sleeping in a corner of the court-yard, the same place his own family chose to sleep. He looked at her puzzled face and her perspiring body and on her lips he could see traces of bread and sugar. He left her and ran into the street, then home. He closed the door, dripping with sweat. His mother had turned off the lights and gone back to sleep, so he went to the dark television room, threw himself down on the colored plastic mat, and rapidly fell into a waking sleep. The taste of sugar in his mouth was still strong and he could still see her at his side. He moved closer until he was touching her soft breasts and could see her childish face like a moon in front of his own face. He kissed her passionately and tasted the sugar in her mouth, and for the first time he felt that he was about to ejaculate. He woke up to a miserable day in soaked clothes and to an intense mixture of happiness and fear. He went back to sleep, anticipating with relish the rare pleasure of the memory.

During this period he took a dislike to the barefoot kids in the neighborhood, perhaps because he wasn't as willing or able as them to fight all the time. The kids would battle endlessly like wild monkeys, in a way that would make him permanently unable to relate to them. They would try to connect with him, but he would not respond.

Perhaps he disliked them also because some of them were delinquent. They had started taking hallucinogenic pills brought by a strange young man from the Manfouha district. One evening Khaled saw a shocking scene with three of the local kids. It was shortly after sunset and he was going out to buy some things from the stationery shop for his sister. On his way from his house to the main street there was a large deserted house before the big hole that had swallowed the child. The house had no door and when he came level to the doorway he heard muffled voices coming from inside. He stopped a moment and made out the voice of the neighbors' son, Mansour. He moved closer to the door and saw Mansour with another boy he knew by sight but not by name. The boy was always coming to their street to visit Mansour. Mansour and his friend had lifted up their thobes and a third boy was standing in front of them, completely naked. They stepped back when they caught sight of him and he went off on his errand, thinking about this scene, which for some reason made him tremble in fear: not disgust, but fear at the idea that one day he might become one of them.

He began adolescence quietly, but with an obvious estrangement from his father. They were not hostile to each other but they constantly disagreed on everything. He began to feel a strong inclination toward writing, and women. He bought a blue notebook and colored pens, and started to write down everything that happened in his life—family events, births in the households of relatives, football matches he attended in the stadium (against his father's wishes), and the heavy rains that always struck fear in their hearts. In the notebook he also stored poems from newspapers and magazines.

He noticed that he had pimples on his face and his voice had broken, and he started to feel embarrassed and flustered merely at a fleeting conversation with a woman. When he began to grow used to this, he noticed that Amira had disappeared from the street. She rarely went out now, and when she came to the doorstep of her house, she would have a pink headscarf on her head. She looked more beautiful and seductive as her breasts began to fill out, and when she met him by chance in the street she would run off home, laughing.

He started to stay away from home for several days with friends from outside the neighborhood, especially in winter, when they would set up camp in the desert outside Riyadh. The man next door had bought his son Walid a small car in which they learned how to drive, and they began to make their way in life. In their encampment they discovered smoking, drinking, and staying up late, and sometimes they brought women along. They drove the car to most of the towns in the country, to Kuwait, and to Basra to drink Iraqi beer and swim in the Shatt al-Arab. That was before the Iran–Iraq War. He always carried with him his private world, his favorite songs, his favorite newspapers. Smoking, drinking, staying up late, and traveling in the summer vacations were part of an incoherent form of rebellion, no more than a desire to distance himself from the monotony of their neighborhood. It was a form of boredom that one evening, when they were in a local coffee shop, made them think of writing petitions in which they would make many demands. But they never put their idea into practice, for the simple reason that in that moment of boredom they decided to go to Kuwait for a frivolous reason—to have leather seat covers fitted in Walid's new car.

His daydreams may have been his only refuge. They were the safe den to which he fled when he was bored with the humdrum and oppressive atmosphere that surrounded his life. It was as if he saw everything proceeding according to strict rules. Even when you were talking with people, you were supposed to say one thing in one situation and not say another thing in another situation; in other words, you had to memorize carefully the way people talked and know how to repeat the right phrases like a parrot, lest it be said that you were not a man. But the daydreams brought him closer to his real self, his uninhibited self. He imagined Riyadh uninhabited except for people he thought closest to his spirit, and he imagined young women always expressing their love for him, just as he dreamed of having another father, and another life filled with Amira and the taste of sugar.

Years earlier, with his head resting on his mother's thigh, half asleep, while his mother was talking with his father and uncles, he asked her, "Does God have a father?" "Shut up, boy," she replied, and he fell asleep.

He never forgot this fragment, and later he would try to guide his memory to other fragments that were more frightening, such as the image of Mansour and his friend and the boy who stripped naked in front of them. He recorded these scenes in his private notebook when he was a little older. At that time his father would speak about many things, and his mother would answer "Praise the Lord! . . . Praise the Lord," while his uncle would talk as if he were preaching in the mosque, to the extent that he told him off sharply when he asked his mother that question about God.

In the television serial the people say "good morning" to each other.

He was puzzled why his family didn't speak the way they spoke on television. He thought that it was only his father who raised his voice in speaking to his mother, until he heard his uncle shouting in her face one day, and at that moment he wanted to hit him. Even the fathers and uncles of the neighbors didn't say "good morning" to each other, and they were always raising their voices in a frightening way.

They all acted differently when rich relatives came to visit. They took exaggerated interest in the visitors and so he felt no affection for these relatives, who seemed like actors on television. He would deliberately do his homework in their presence, so that they knew he was as educated as them.

He always filled his notebooks with the best pictures, and with writings he would copy verbatim from newspapers and magazines.

At the dining table the real problems began:

"Why don't you eat like a human being?"

Or: "Did you say grace, you donkey?"

In the mosque, after afternoon prayers, the sheikh was preaching, a sheikh they knew. He came from outside the neighborhood, and the children started playing around while listening to him. Sometimes the kids would exchange little glances and laugh, and suddenly he received a slap on the back of the neck from behind. He looked back to see who had hit him, but he couldn't tell. All those behind him were fathers, and if they were fathers they were bound to hit.

He thought: *All of us are like that: we and the neighbors, and the neighbors' relatives. We offer smiles and polite language only to outsiders, while we insult and hit each other. Talking about politics is banned because the walls have ears.*

Fear . . . of everything . . .

Once his sister came into his room with his brother. Khaled played them a new tape and gave them some children's magazines.

His father came in. "Teach them the basics of Islam, you good-for-nothing."

His little brother asked him, "Is singing forbidden?"

Khaled answered, "When you've completed your education and passed your exams, read the traditions of the Prophet and you can find out for yourself."

When Khaled was at university, he received a monthly allowance from the government. His father was too embarrassed to take it. He told Khaled, "I don't need your allowance."

Khaled wondered, "So was he thinking of taking it?"

Then his father started to grow old and sick.

And his sister Afaf grew into a pretty adolescent.

And his brother Ahmad entered a world of religious delusions.

They all grew older, perhaps in a single moment. It wasn't a moment in time, but it left its marks on the walls of the place.

With his allowance he started to pay installments on a small car, as his friend had done. He had learned to drive with him. His father was angry. "Why didn't you tell me? Why didn't you take me with you?" he said, while his mother said, "Congratulations."

Another time his brother came home carrying a piece of cloth dripping with mud. His mother ran up and took it from him. "Where did you find that, boy?" "Next to the door," he said. His mother put on her gown, put the piece of cloth in a bag, and went out. Ahmad ran after her, asking, "Where are you going, Mama?" She called him, he ran after her, and they reached that hole, the remains of the old well in which lay the body of the child who had accidentally fallen in. She threw the piece of cloth into the depths of the hole as she recited verses of the Quran. When they were home, she told them, "These things are magic spells meant to drive us apart." Sitting in the courtyard in her gown, she gave a sigh and said, "Infidels!"

He felt sorry for her at that moment. He would have liked to hug her and kiss her head, and he didn't know why he didn't do so. The same thing happened when he met his father after a long absence and felt that something stood between them, although he knew that he wanted his father. Afaf was shocked by the cloth incident.

One Friday afternoon he heard that Mansour, the neighbors' son, had killed himself. He didn't believe it at first. The last time he had seen Mansour was with the other two boys in the big deserted house that stood just before the main street, when Mansour was half-naked.

He was walking toward their house when he heard the news, so he walked on to investigate the incident. As he strolled down the street, a street full of memories, with his feet he traced pictures like music in the dust. He walked slowly with his eyes on the ground, tracing first one deep line, then another line crossing it, then a circle and some scattered dots, building a melody that reflected the rhythm of time and the intense impressions left by certain images, some discouraging and some exciting. He didn't understand what many of the stories that circulated in their neighborhood meant. Sometimes he thought they were just figments of a wild imagination. Did it make sense that this long street he walked down every day should hold stories that gave rise to such fear, such sadness, such pain, and also such sympathy?

They were talking about Mansour, the young man they had heard so much about and had rarely seen. He was like a legend from ancient times. They said that on the evening of the previous Friday he had set fire to himself and reduced their house to a pile of ash, that they took the boy to the hospital hovering between life and death, and that he finally passed away there.

Why?

No one knew . . . because houses hold secrets . . . .

He reached the house of the young rebel (his sister called him "poor" and his mother called him "criminal"), with his eyes to the ground and his feet tracing pictures in the dust. *This is their house, but where's the pile of ash they're talking about?* Nothing about the house had changed. He stood in front of the door for a while, in case one of them came out and he could see the pile of ash inside. He was waiting for the door to open when Mansour's father came along carrying a bag of bread and a bag of oranges. He opened the door, went in quickly, and left the door open for his other son to come in after him. Khaled looked into the hallway and, at the top of the wall above a curtain, he could see black marks that might have been traces of a fire, or could be . . . he wasn't sure. He tried to work out what had happened. The pile of ash was now just black lines. Yes, there had been a fire, but maybe it wasn't intentional. He headed back, unable to connect what he had heard and what he had seen. Hearing a movement behind him, he turned. He saw Mansour's little sister stick her head out to call her other brother. She had her usual plaits and her eyes twinkled like a bird's. Her little red nose made her face look like a cat's. Their eyes met, he smiled at her, and just before she went back into the house she stuck out her red tongue, then smiled mischievously and disappeared. He went back to his own street, telling himself that this last image of a cat's face was better than a pile of ash.

Back on his little street, he thought of many things, such as why people try to kill themselves. He remembered that Mansour was mentally ill and had suffered greatly before he died. Mansour never liked school, and everyone would hit him, at home and at school, but in return he would hit everyone in the neighborhood.

Had he really died? Was there really a fire? How could that have happened when Mansour's sister was still up to her usual tricks, sticking her tongue out at passersby and laughing?

He saw his friend Walid sitting on the neighbors' back doorstep, with his sleeves rolled up and his thobe lifted up above his knees, holding a large slice of watermelon to his mouth. The juice ran down his face. Still puzzled, Khaled sat next to him and told him the whole story, including the unanswered questions, but Walid asked him, "Who told you Mansour was dead?"

"*She* did," he answered.

"Who's 'she'?"

"My sister."

"Shut up," said Walid. "Mansour died in another incident." Glancing around he added, "I'll tell you later."

Walid was flustered and Khaled was as puzzled as ever. He started imagining other versions of how Mansour, the famous boy rebel, had died—versions that would set the scene far away from his house, which had not in fact turned into a pile of ash, and that would include the cat's face, to which he had taken a liking, and that was enough for him. He left Walid on the doorstep and went on walking down the lane like a drunken ship, tossing and turning in every direction, with only sad fish inside it, and an overpowering scent of lemon started to fill the lane.

He walked along the road alone, his loose thobe blowing in the welcome breeze. As he walked he tried to catch hold of the memories that now came in full spate, in rhythm with the afternoon sun, which tinged the walls of the houses the color of lemon.

He walked slowly, stirring the lifeless dust with his feet.

This was a road he had known for years; the road where he had learned to walk and talk.

From here he would come out on what they called Black Street, now a silent street that had lost its cheerful hustle and bustle. Where had all the people gone and how had the street lost its vitality so suddenly?

There had been a time when he believed that all the world's inhabitants lived on Black Street, the street of songs.

It was the throbbing heart of the neighborhood, a gauge of its joys and sorrows.

Every Thursday morning he would get up early, come down from the dusty roof where the whole family went to sleep every evening, and run off there—to the street of fun and of people, a long street with houses side by side and full of humanity. Every house had a story, and every story was the starting point for a novel.

In those days the young men of the street painted the walls of their houses white, but the local children then covered the white walls with the words of famous songs, written in black, and its name became Black Street or Song Street.

At the beginning of the street there lived a real-estate dealer they never saw, with a fat, pale wife who sold hairpieces and cosmetics to the local women. She had a clever daughter who had a modern radio of which she took great care and on which she played songs at high volume most evenings. The real estate agent died and his wife started buying up the houses in the neighborhood, one after another, in competition with Sheikh Ibrahim. Eventually she came to their house, but Khaled's grandfather refused to bargain with her. She told him, "The housing bank will offer you a loan to live in the new suburbs and the mud-brick houses will lose value." But his grandfather constantly refused. Then Sheikh Ibrahim came and bought up the neighborhood, ran the mosque, and took on the office of mayor . . . and everything else.

At the other end of the street lived a rice and sugar merchant who grew rich and took three wives—one from Riyadh, one from Egypt, and a third from Syria. He was very proud of his pure Arab blood. His wives bore him twenty children, and the man stopped talking to people and started walking round the streets talking to himself.

In the middle of the narrow street there lived a civil servant who worked at the municipality and married a young woman who bore him many boys and girls. He fought with them every day like a rooster, and when he tired of them he went up to the roof of his house and trained the pigeons in his pigeon loft to fly long distance.

Khaled now felt that the whole place was like a chronicle of myths remembered, of old sorrows. The street was like a language adrift.

The street of songs had lost its voice, because the real-estate dealer's wife was no longer fat and white, the mud-brick houses she had bought had lost their value, and she no longer sold hairpieces and cosmetics to the local women. Her clever daughter's radio had broken, she no longer listened to music, and she had started to become withdrawn. The sugar merchant's children did not do well at school, the man with all the boys and girls lost his pigeons on long flights, and the era of Sheikh Ibrahim the real-estate dealer had begun.

He walked slowly up and down the streets and lanes, thinking of that rounded face. He still remembered some details of his childhood, and he clutched the memories in his fist, together with an old fear, a tiredness, disappointments, and fragments of songs that dropped into the dust behind him as he walked along with an overworked memory, sick at heart.

He went back home and his mother greeted him with the news that they were going to move the next month to the new house that his father had finished building in the Badia district. His mother was delighted at the prospect of leaving the small mud house for a spacious villa, but she was also thinking of her brothers and sisters, who had moved out to other districts. She started to sense the dissolution of the bonds that held them together in this neighborhood. Khaled received the news with indifference, because he had already made up his mind to rent an apartment, but also to keep a room for himself in his family's new house so that they would not feel they had lost him, and he would not feel he had lost them.

He was preoccupied with thoughts about the notebook in which he recorded events, memories, and dreams, and the image that most excited him was the most secret one. When he was going to his room in the house or out into the street, he would have in his mind recurrent images of a beautiful girl fully naked. Although he disapproved of this habit, he could not escape it. The images might have many faces, but the faces of Amira and of the girl in the bakery were the dominant ones. Sometimes the idea of suicide seemed tempting, but he quickly dispelled it, preferring to console himself with the pleasure of imagining the body of a naked woman, especially before he went to sleep, when he would imagine, for example, that he was lying on his back with an erection, with a beautiful girl on top of him, waiting for him to embrace her.

He often speculated about his relationship with Amira. Was it love? He quite simply didn't know, but he began to fight off the idea of imagining her naked in front of him. Sometimes he would tell himself that this was because of his respect and love for her, and sometimes he would tell himself that he was supposed to see her as his sister, so for weeks he would fall prey to this inner conflict. He would buy books and spend much time reading, but he couldn't find what he was looking for because the best books, which he read about in magazines, weren't available in the bookshops. He had pangs of conscience that alarmed him and gave rise to doubts, because he didn't know what had happened to him that dark night. Had something happened or not? Did she know what had happened or not? Endless questions that on many occasions made his days an unbearable hell.

Amira was a sad fish like his sister Afaf. That's what he wrote at the end of his private notebook.

Another Place

THE MORNING BLAZED EARLY that day. Khaled woke to a sky that radiated scorching heat and went out to the street to wait, in the hopes of glimpsing her pretty face seeing them off to their new neighborhood. He stood on the doorstep by the wooden door, happy as a lark. He went out into the lane in case she was there. She might look out at them; she might hear their voices in the lane and appear. Now her face dominated everything he saw. She might come out now and sit on the doorstep of her house, put her hand on her cheek, and watch the joys, sorrows, and dreams of their ailing neighborhood. In conversation one evening she said everything, and he said everything, and the most beautiful thing said was what the expression on her face said, and on his face he could still feel the bountiful light that shone from her eyes.

Walid came by, put a glass of arak down beside him, and moved on. Khaled drank from it and put the glass down again. At the bottom of the glass, alongside the mint leaf, he saw many faces. He would say goodbye to her before they left for the new world that awaited them. He had often walked along this lane in the months before they moved out. Then the time to leave came, after many years that had left their mark on the walls of these good and honest houses. Khaled felt that something new and mysterious wanted to speak up in this dark lane, and he still didn't know the answer to the question: *Do we like this neighborhood or hate it? And whose neighborhood will it be after we leave?*

Khaled's father awoke from a long sleep. He got out of bed and felt lethargic, with aching limbs. Going to the bathroom, he stood in front of the mirror, resting on his stick. He noticed that the dizziness he usually felt when he woke up had stopped, and he thanked God. He looked at his gray beard and the eyes that suggested many trials and tribulations. He could hear his wife talking to another woman and repeating, "Inshallah, inshallah." The other woman, whose voice he did not recognize, was telling his wife, "Wipe his neck and chest with a towel soaked in Quran water." He could hear the voices of the two women clearly. They were talking about his son Ahmad and suddenly, for a fleeting moment, he felt he had heard the same rapid conversation before and that he was living exactly the same moment for a second time, although he knew that was impossible. He put his head under the tap and turned it on, and the sudden feeling disappeared. He turned the tap off, put a towel on his head and left the bathroom, wondering what he would do in the new neighborhood, far from the office of Sheikh Ibrahim the real estate man, after growing accustomed to his neighbors for so many years. He spread out his prayer mat and prayed, listening to the voices outside—his wife and children moving furniture out to the truck. He still felt that life had lost its appeal since the first signs of what they called the economic boom, which had granted people loans to build new houses in the new suburbs. The first indication of this boom came when his neighbor bought his young son a new car, which he drove around the neighborhood as if it were a toy. The image stuck in his mind because it wasn't till he was past sixty, just three years ago, that he had been able to buy a used car, but now the children were driving small cars down the narrow streets. A real upheaval had taken place in the world. And then there were the constant increases in the prices of everything. Could he afford all this on his modest monthly salary?

Khaled's mother opened her big steel trunk and it gave off a smell of dust. Inside there were small bags of herbs, a square jar of honey her brother had brought from Turkey, and a small radio that had faded from brown to white, with a torn leather cover. Khaled's father had once followed all the news on it, but with the advent of television the radio lost its value and became a treasured antique that his mother preserved. She sat in front of the trunk and searched through her old clothes. A photograph fell out and she picked it up and saw herself surrounded by her children in the neighbors' garden. She kissed her children, then kissed herself and laughed. She began to gather her things together in readiness to move them to the truck waiting in front of the house.

Now the local children were hovering around the truck that would carry the family's furniture. Many neighboring families had already moved to the dream world. The only ones left were a few who were still waiting for the boom to give them a chance to leave these narrow streets and their dilapidated mud houses.

The children from the small streets nearby were the same children who in past years used to hover around the donkey carts that stopped in front of their houses to unload sacks of rice, sugar, tea, and other foodstuffs, after the decades of hunger their families had survived in the towns and villages of Najd. The children had seen the last of those decades in their impoverished childhoods, but the transition carried a heavy price that they paid throughout their lives, including a psychological price by breaking up communities.

At this historic moment a real truck, not a donkey cart, had stopped in front of their house, and they were about to move to the promised land, but Khaled's head was still full of nagging questions about the new world they would move to. Who would their neighbors be and how would they talk? How would they live? Would they sleep on the roof of the villa or would they get used to sleeping in air-conditioned rooms? Would they, for example, eat at a table, like the people they saw on television, rather than on mats on the floor? Many questions, with answers yet unknown.

He now began to smell a new smell after the dirt road was sprinkled with water—a strong smell that seemed to coat the walls that morning with fresh colors. The smell evoked a mixture of happiness, fear, and anticipation, accompanied by a faint sense, somewhere deep in his memory, that it was not he who was about to leave the lane, but someone else. He still didn't believe he was going to move away, and after all those years he wondered whose lane it would become.

At that moment Omar, the young man who lived next door, passed by and asked after Khaled's brother Ahmad.

"He's inside," Khaled answered.

"So where are you off to?" Omar asked, looking at the truck.

"To our new house, as you can see," he said.

"Congratulations," said Omar.

"Thanks," he answered.

Omar walked on, and Khaled watched the young man, bearded and wearing a short thobe, as he strode off. He remembered him as a boy two years ago, when he would see him waiting his turn at the bakery every morning. He was cheerful and popular then, good-looking, with a sense of humor. Now he and Ahmad talked only about

what was right and wrong, although they were still adolescents. Their problem began when they failed to graduate
from middle school and some of the dropouts turned to
religion, while others adopted a life of travel and drugs
and took that to the limit. Khaled remembered how his
father once told Ahmad irritably, "We knew God before
you were born," and told him to give up his religious
fanaticism. Then he turned to Khaled as if reproaching
him for his life of late nights and escapism.

His sister Afaf came out of the house carrying her
big black suitcase, with her Walkman in her hand, playing
light music. She had indeed grown up and had her own
private things. She put her suitcase in the truck and
winked at him as he sat on the neighbors' doorstep. She
gave a fleeting smile: she was the happiest of them all
to be leaving the district.

He remembered her as a girl with a short ponytail,
in the morning on school holidays, running with them
to Riyadh's noisy old market when it was full of women
in black gowns—women selling bread, dates, pigeons,
amulets, and fabric. In the market, men and women
would tell each other old stories. They offered powdered
substances to treat the sick, in bags or old tin cans that
smelled of henna, anise, or fenugreek. The women would
also read verses of the Quran over the sick, and blow puffs
of air from their healthy lungs onto their sick chests.

The moving truck was full and they set off ahead of
it. Along the way, he had many misgivings. He saw their

house disappear behind them—not just the place, but also the faces, the events, and the images. He saw many things tumbling down behind him—memories, dreams, songs, joys, and sorrows, a history crowded with images receding into the distance in a moment of clarity.

They reached the house of dreams and unloaded the furniture with hesitant glee. But there was no one around them—no voices, no neighbors, just a few children sitting politely on their doorsteps. The neighbors' houses were still, with towering walls.

They took the furniture in and the truck left. They started to put things in place until they were exhausted, and then they fell asleep in the living room, with furniture dispersed around them.

He woke up early and spent all the time in his new room, a real room with painted walls, a whole room he need not share with anyone, a room with a glass window. He tipped the details of his life out into the middle of it and started to put everything in place, even his memory. He decided to put it temporarily in one of the cupboards until he could put the pieces back together.

A Soul Departs

IT WAS HIS FATHER who felt most uncomfortable, but with the passage of time he started to get used to the new place. Every weekend, however, he would ask his son to drive him to their old neighborhood. Khaled would drop him off in front of Sheikh Ibrahim's real estate office every Thursday afternoon and come back after evening prayers.

Relatives stopped visiting his mother except on important occasions, but she made friends with her new neighbors, and his brother Ahmad would still meet up with young men in the local mosque or stay away from home for days on end. Then the young men started printing booklets telling people what was right and wrong, and put the loudspeakers at the mosque on maximum volume, perhaps to assert their existence.

Meanwhile his sister Afaf closed herself up in her room and spent her time doing her homework, sleeping, or chatting to her girlfriends on the phone, until she got married. Thus the winds of change swept them away: silence, monotony, and boredom replaced the hustle and bustle and the visits with neighbors and relatives, not just because the new suburbs were so far apart but because people's lives had changed, not on the inside but on the outside. Almost everyone started running to keep abreast of the economic changes. The streets were full of small business ventures: restaurants, workshops, tailors, video shops, small apartment blocks. The houses were full of knickknacks from all over the world and people boasted about them as if they had made them themselves.

He noticed how Riyadh had become a hive of activity without producing anything real and without the most basic elements of real life. Everyone was constantly running, but they didn't know where they were going. Young men chased breathlessly after business with no guarantee of success, but other young men didn't like the tedium and turned to religion, filling their spare time with promoting virtue and preventing vice. Amazing stories began to emerge from this soulless life; they started to hear that business ventures had failed, that many people had gone bankrupt and their dreams were ruined, while others had become rich, prominent, and influential, all at the whim of chance, which either put you at the top of the ladder or threw you down to the bottom. In the newspapers he would read of governments in southeast Asia whose countries were booming, while here you didn't know where you stood in spite of all this wealth. People competed to travel abroad, buy land, and build mansions, or just to promote virtue and prevent vice. That's all they knew.

Khaled went to work in the morning and came home at three in the afternoon. He would put the newspapers aside and sit down to have lunch with his family. Then he'd go up to his room, change his clothes, and try to sleep. Mostly he would stay awake, tossing in bed for more than an hour. This often happened in the months after they moved to the new house, and so he started to go to his own apartment in midafternoon and sometimes sleep there.

One dusty afternoon he woke up in the family home a little before sunset and saw that the air in this city of masks had turned full circle, once, twice, and a third time. The dust that had long lain still stirred and started to chase after the small spiraling gusts of air. The circle widened and the dust rose to form a red pillar that filled much of the vast sky on the edge of the city, driven by a wind that was brutal and increasingly frenzied. It spun like a woman looking for a lost love. The air raged in the depths of the city, pounding it from all sides, as if it wanted to swallow the city up with a shrill whistling, angry and harsh. The dust fell in abundance on the stunned residents, coating the roofs of the houses and mosques, shrouding the city in darkness, then moving on, crossing the streets and the pavements, the lanes and people's faces, covering the walls, the trees, and the ancestral tombs, covering everything, driven by some obscure malignant impulse. Men and women scurried home like panicked mice, closing their doors and windows in terrified unison. God's overpowering wrath descended on the good city, and only the children dared to go out, slipping covertly out of their parents' houses and running through the lanes as if they were honoring the city's guest in a carnival of joy, celebrating freedom and the thrill of fear, dancing in the lanes for the stranger who had come to their city pleading that they change their ways. The children ran through the streets and along the walls, relishing the transformation of their humdrum world into something new and exciting, as if they were at a wedding that could last thousands of years. The wind headed south, taking the city's dust with it and clearing some of it from the disk of the sun. In its awesome departure it looked like the devil's bride. The children cleared the dust out of their hair, their clothes, and the throats that carried their old voices, and sprinkled water on the dust that had started to settle in front of their timorous doors. They kneaded the mud again, remembered their old names and their dates of birth, and traced them on the walls—the walls that had become lustrous under a sun that was brilliant and new, for a new phase.

When the storm died down, he went in to his father, who put the newspaper aside and set his glasses on top of it.

"It's left the capital and things have calmed down," Khaled told him.

"We're still in the eye of the storm," his father replied, "and I don't think things will come to an end."

He began to feel that his father was really sick, because he was coughing frequently and breathing slowly.

"Let's go see the doctors," Khaled said.

"Not now."

"Why not?"

"I'm better now. Tomorrow's Thursday and we'll take the workers to finish off the work on your grandfather's house."

On Thursday morning he took his father and they went to their old house. Sheikh Ibrahim had brought the workers and they had been digging and building since early morning. His father stayed, monitoring their work, till midafternoon. Then he felt tired, so he lay down on a piece of cardboard and fell asleep. Khaled tried to wake him up a few minutes later but he didn't respond. At once Khaled called Sheikh Ibrahim, who came with some neighbors who happened to be in his office. They took him to the hospital, where he spent three days on an artificial respirator and then died; his soul went to his Creator's Heaven quietly and peacefully.

The next afternoon mourners descended on their house to pay their condolences. They came from parts of old Riyadh and from their village—people his father had worked with for many years. At the mourning ceremony

Khaled was silent as people offered their condolences to him, to his brother, and to his mother's brothers. One of them said, "He was a righteous man, may he rest in peace," and another replied, "Praise the Lord, who takes unto Himself only the righteous." Khaled used to laugh at this last expression, but this time he controlled himself and wondered, *What if God really did take only the righteous? Where would that leave those who remained, and how would they get along?* The condolences went on three days and they came to know the neighbors in the district, then calm returned to the house.

His younger brother Ahmad went off to Afghanistan and they lost contact with him. So Khaled didn't go to his apartment for several weeks but spent his time between work and the family home. He tried to be closer to his mother, though his mother's sister was also there. She had decided to stay in their house after her husband died and her sons and daughters got married. Then he tired of the daily routine, and one Thursday morning, he decided to take the curtain off his bedroom window, fill the room with light and incense, turn on the tape player, turn the volume up, and raise his voice and dance. He went into the bathroom and came out elated. He dressed, singing along with Abdel Halim Hafez. He closed his eyes, and took a swig of arak from the same old glass—the cup with the mint leaf that he knew. Then he left his room like a bird, kissed his mother on the head, and kissed his sister Afaf, who had come to visit them with her little boy. He said goodbye to them as if he were traveling, went out to the street and drove off to his safe den, far from the stealthy faces and the suspicious looks that lay in wait for everyone. Out in the open, he filled his lungs with fresh air, then went back to his apartment, enjoying the darkness and quiet.

That was the day Iraq under Saddam Hussein decided to be an unwelcome guest in Kuwait.

Then the images came thick and fast—the marches with religious slogans, the emotional protests by women demanding the right to drive, as if the pressure cooker needed an invasion of some kind in order to let off steam, and finally the image of Baghdad being bombed—an event that made everyone hold their breath, and the first step toward an overt occupation of the whole region.

A Mysterious Image

NO ONE ASKS about anything in this Riyadh.

This city's people are used to its monotony, to its indifference, to its strident silence, to the fact that the walls have ears.

A deep silence that makes everything the same.

Khaled lived face to face with the bustle of the streets and the houses: a coarse, meaningless noise in a city that doesn't know if it's pious or decadent, a city that doesn't say what it thinks and feels, a city that sleeps on a huge pile of words not yet uttered, a silencer-city like a pressure cooker in which the smell has long been brewing. The smell wants to escape and maybe people know that eventually some smell will spread through the city air, exposing what was hidden when they piled up the words and slept on top of them.

Do I love this Riyadh or hate it?

Am I lucky here or unlucky?

The questions reminded him of his religious studies teacher: the lucky go to heaven and the unlucky go to hell. The lucky listen to the word of God while the unlucky listen to the word of Satan.

But this fanatical teacher would open a packet of cigarettes behind the school wall, smoke one, and come back for another class, repeating the lucky/unlucky lesson as he rubbed his thighs against the edge of the first table in the class throughout the lesson.

The teacher once caught one of the boys smoking a delicious first cigarette far down the small lane behind the mosque. "Smoking! Smoking, you son of a whore! If your father knew . . ." the teacher shouted in his face.

After the incident Khaled kept speculating about the link between smoking and fornication. Was smoking fornication, or was the sheikh just rude? But the word 'fornication' buzzed in his head like a catchy new tune. It buzzed for a long time, and he wanted to swat it like a fly. Meanwhile the pangs of conscience, the image of young Amira, the fear and his lapses of memory tortured his sick being.

After he found a job and rented a small apartment, and his family settled into the new villa, he didn't expect to receive such a torrent of friendly phone calls from women. He didn't expect the apartment would open up to him the secrets of Riyadh's underworld. In the beginning, when he was at school and university, he was a dreamy idealist. After he graduated he remained so in his conversations with the women who called, and, as the psychological barriers between him and them gradually crumbled, he began to approach them with a shyness that betrayed a deep desire. Then the barriers came down entirely, and the warm voices kept pouring in from everywhere and his life was full of girls of all kinds. After two years of anarchy, he carried out a purge and only three remained. He would make bets with himself on whether they loved him, especially Nujoud, who started to look after him as if she were his wife. She would come every Thursday afternoon, clean the apartment for him and stay up late with him, then go home. As for the other girls, who came from the lower world of Khazzan Street, he broke ties with them forever, after a long examination of his conscience.

Nujoud was a divorcee in her thirties with one boy. He had met her by chance in a shopping center. He didn't take much interest in her at first because he saw her as snobbish, but after a time, when he came to know her well, he realized that she was a genuine and simple human being who concealed her anger and her sense of alienation from her family. They began to meet frequently.

He would buy the newspapers daily and enjoyed reading them every morning. He sometimes thought of writing or painting but he was never in the right mood. He would say repeatedly that smoking and eating were the best work in this country. After that he began to buy only one newspaper, just enough so as not to be cut off from the world. He would read it hurriedly, especially after he tired of the headlines and the repetitive articles.

He wanted to write only to stimulate his memory, as the doctor had prescribed, so that he would not one day become a man without a memory or someone who has to count from one to ten.

The months and years passed in deep silence. There were visits to relatives and friends, and then sudden ruptures. Everyone drowned in the whirlpool of life, tossing and turning as they sank. Every year he ran off to some Arab capital. He would carry his chronic illnesses everywhere with him. He would go for many reasons, but when he was there he would merely stay up late, sleep, then come back.

He had phases of anxiety, accompanied by a clear feeling that the dream house, the dream family, the dream job, and his dreams of the theater had all come to nothing. He began to wonder why his brother had died in Afghanistan, why Mansour, their old neighbor, had killed himself, and why he had moments when he toyed with the idea of suicide himself, as though he were taking his own pulse. He came to see his brother's death in Afghanistan as linked to Mansour's suicide and as part of his own wretched state as he now tried to look for Amira whatever the circumstances, in order to arrange in one complete sequence all the images of his life, in all its mystery and uncertainty.

The images included the image of the husband of his poor sister Afaf.

Afaf's husband was distant, optimistic, and straight as a ruler. He spent his time sleeping, eating, and working, as though he had no part in the busy world around him. Sometimes Khaled envied him, and sometimes he pitied him, because the man would go to bed at nine o'clock and wake up at six in the morning, have breakfast, and go to work. He would come back to have lunch and take a nap. Sometimes he would come home from work just to have sex, then go back to work again. He loved the government and he loved money even more, and women too. He thought that everything was perfect, just as he read in the newspapers, and that we didn't give God the thanks He deserved. He also thought that Israel was God's scourge to test the faith of Muslims. Every Friday afternoon he would go to the car auction and buy a car, then sell it the following week after making some improvements. So he came to have two incomes, but at home he lived like a pauper and rumors of his miserliness circulated in the streets nearby. He listened to music and then would say it was sinful. In summer he went to Morocco and left his wife and daughter with her family. Then he tired of this way of life and grew a beard and adopted a new style, full of religious admonitions and preaching virtue. Now he hated the government but still loved women, so the flame of Afaf's spirit blew out and she devoted her life to her house and her daughter, whose eyes suggested she had the same gifts as her mother.

Would her daughter be smothered too, like a small, pathetic flame, before it has time to give light? That was the question Khaled asked the last time he visited Afaf's house.

Every weekend his friend Walid would come and visit, and they would spend Thursday and Friday together, but their meetings had lost the warmth of previous get-togethers. Friends had grown apart and things had calmed down. People were busier than ever after the spread of satellite channels, mobile phones, coffee shops, and large shopping malls.

Maybe life is a set of consecutive images, linked only by what we try to create in our relationships with each other.

That was what he concluded when he remembered Amira. *Where was she now?* Had she married a man as distant as Afaf's husband, or did she have a man friend like his Nujoud?

He asked his sister about Amira, and she said, "I heard they're living in the next neighborhood, after her divorce." "Does she have any children?" he asked. "I don't know," she replied. Afaf's daughter was following their conversation with her little sparkling eyes. He exchanged a fleeting glance with the girl and he said to himself, *I'm still living a life on hold*.

In this way he saw life as a succession of demises.

His father snuffed out by death, his brother by suicide in Afghanistan, his sister by marriage, Amira by divorce, his mother by the diseases of old age. He himself had become a memory about to be forgotten, but the taste of sugar on his tongue was still strong, giving him a faint sense of optimism about life, and warding off temporarily the specter of suicide.

The Sound of Silence

IN RARE MOMENTS a sudden desire to cry, like a flash of lightning but as deep as the ocean, would take him by surprise, and he would ask of this painful desire: "Why don't you come more often and linger a while, so that I can grasp some of your secrets?"

An incandescent voice from the past intruded every evening and told Khaled in a whisper, "Be who you are, and no one else."

Now he felt as if he was looking at the world through a small hole in the wall of his silent house. The darkness was growing more intense and he could hear their conversations clearly. They stopped talking for a while, then suddenly their conversations resumed from somewhere else in the house, perhaps from the sitting room or the hall, and he could see a faint light moving sometimes in various places.

He found himself in a very tight spot, in front of the window open to the great outside. The space began to close in on him, stifled by the smoke of his cigarette. His limbs fell limp at his sides. He looked up at the wooden cupboard in the hall in the distance. He remembered his papers, his books, and the little projects he had put on hold. His dreams faded out for a while and he could hear the people quietly leaving his house, one after another, and he could see that he had turned into a small hole in an old wall, looking for his limbs, which had disappeared. He felt he was about to evaporate drop by drop. The feeling had begun the moment he was born and continued up to now. He heard a faint wheeze coming from the innermost depths of his chest, and this gave him intimations of mortality—dreams unfulfilled, struggles postponed, beautiful things in ruins, questions unanswered, and the relics of an old fear of all fathers, of the future, and of pangs of conscience.

For the thousandth time he was overcome by a desire for silence and to be at one with the silence of the things around him. When he was angry, he wanted to break with all the old traditions. *I want to listen to beautiful music that will take me back to my childhood, or to when I was a lovesick youth, or a traveler in long exile, or a wanderer who has lost his bearings in the desert. I want to sleep as still as the birds, without dreaming or burdening my head with details.*

I need a life that is noble and free, deep and calm, a woman who runs with me when I want to run in all directions and stays with me when I want to go back to my isolated corner, a friend who doesn't stab me in the back, and a pen with which to record my victories and my defeats.

I want to be a painting, a question, a dream, a child lost in the streets of a vast city looking for an ancient woman to teach him how to be as clear as water and as pure as the hearts of the poor.

He once watched his worries as they hovered over the office table. They didn't take the risk of landing, nor the risk of flying high. They were like bashful little clouds, sniffing out the air of the room and asking: "What diseases are you bequeathing to your children, you depraved people?"

In bouts of restless sleep he saw the depraved with their hungry red eyes, devouring the streets. He saw them counting people's money and making fun of them, stealing everything in sight. Then one unpleasant evening he saw them multiplying around him and he woke up in a panic and threw them out of his bedroom.

In these bouts of restless sleep some of the voices that came to him were frightening, brazen, and melancholy. The voices came from afar, woke him up, and took him off to see his parents and his ancestors as they roamed his little streets. They looked at the expressions on the faces of the local people and wondered how they were, and he could see that deep desire for silence invading his life, so that he could retrieve an image, still blurred, of the little house he had abandoned. It still bore the traces of children: drawings on white paper, of palm trees, tents, blue streams, a lute, pencils, a place, and then a star that had been spinning in the middle of the room for a long time, and on the other wall distant faces walking across a vast desert, and the footsteps of the pre-Islamic poets of Najd, unburied by the winds.

He wanted to sleep as still as the birds, dreaming of nothing, not burdening his head with the details, every day reading and writing new songs about an old taste of sugar that was still on his tongue.

When the pages of his blue notebook were full, he found that the music, the catchy tune that was stuck in his head, rode roughshod over the individual words, that silence was the master of the situation, that fear was squatting in every corner, planting suspicions in everyone's mind, and that the elusive truth he had been chasing was still elusive.

He put aside the pages of music, the sadness and the questions, and went out into the street looking for the missing fields and for the lanes that looked like drunken ships, surrounded by sad blind fish.

Then he wrote his unfulfilled dreams on the walls. On the pebbles of Najd's ancient roads he wrote the unanswered questions, and he wrote the dedication to his sister Afaf.

"No, Afaf, I'm not sick," he told his sister on the phone. "I merely choke on my saliva sometimes when

I'm asleep. I wake up in a panic and drink half the glass of water that's next to me, and go back to sleep." He laughed and added, "But are you still a sad fish?"

"Yes," she laughed.

"You were the first person to point out the song 'Where Are the Millions?' to me. Do you remember . . . ? I'm coming to you," he said.

He headed toward the western part of Riyadh:

Maybe I'm not sick. It's true that my memory has improved, but I'm still restless when I sleep, and I can live with my anxiety. Do you understand, Afaf? After that I'll get over the dark days, then think of marrying, as you would like me to. I have to adapt properly to their way of life.

Do you understand, Afaf? We are not just blind, sad fish; we are all creatures on hold. I don't want to die now, I want to stay with you, the most beautiful woman in the world, a creature on hold.

He went out to the street confused, lifted up his hands, and looked at his fingernails. In them he could still see an image of his father wandering down the lanes, along the old tracks. He bowed his head and made his submission to life, as the idea of the soul separating from the body rang deep inside his mind.

Betool Khedairi *Absent*
Mohammed Khudayyir *Basrayatha*
Ibrahim al-Koni *Anubis • Gold Dust • The Puppet • The Seven Veils of Seth*
Naguib Mahfouz *Adrift on the Nile • Akhenaten: Dweller in Truth*
Arabian Nights and Days • Autumn Quail • Before the Throne • The Beggar
The Beginning and the End • Cairo Modern • The Cairo Trilogy: Palace Walk
Palace of Desire • Sugar Street • Children of the Alley • The Coffeehouse
The Day the Leader Was Killed • The Dreams • Dreams of Departure
Echoes of an Autobiography • The Essential Naguib Mahfouz • The Final Hour
The Harafish • Heart of the Night • In the Time of Love
The Journey of Ibn Fattouma • Karnak Cafe • Khan al-Khalili • Khufu's Wisdom
Life's Wisdom • Love in the Rain • Midaq Alley • The Mirage • Miramar • Mirrors
Morning and Evening Talk • Naguib Mahfouz at Sidi Gaber • Respected Sir
Rhadopis of Nubia • The Search • The Seventh Heaven • Thebes at War
The Thief and the Dogs • The Time and the Place • Voices from the Other World
Wedding Song • The Wisdom of Naguib Mahfouz
Mohamed Makhzangi *Memories of a Meltdown*
Alia Mamdouh *The Loved Ones • Naphtalene*
Selim Matar *The Woman of the Flask*
Ibrahim al-Mazini *Ten Again*
Yousef Al-Mohaimeed *Munira's Bottle • Wolves of the Crescent Moon*
Hassouna Mosbahi *A Tunisian Tale*
Ahlam Mosteghanemi *Chaos of the Senses • Memory in the Flesh*
Shakir Mustafa *Contemporary Iraqi Fiction: An Anthology*
Mohamed Mustagab *Tales from Dayrut*
Buthaina Al Nasiri *Final Night*
Ibrahim Nasrallah *Inside the Night • Time of White Horses*
Haggag Hassan Oddoul *Nights of Musk*
Mona Prince *So You May See*
Mohamed Mansi Qandil *Moon over Samarqand*
Abd al-Hakim Qasim *Rites of Assent*
Somaya Ramadan *Leaves of Narcissus*
Kamal Ruhayyim *Days in the Diaspora*
Mahmoud Saeed *The World through the Eyes of Angels*
Mekkawi Said *Cairo Swan Song*
Ghada Samman *The Night of the First Billion*
Mahdi Issa al-Saqr *East Winds, West Winds*
Rafik Schami *The Calligrapher's Secret • Damascus Nights • The Dark Side of Love*
Habib Selmi *The Scents of Marie-Claire*
Khairy Shalaby *The Hashish Waiter • The Lodging House*
Khalil Sweileh *Writing Love*
The Time-Travels of the Man Who Sold Pickles and Sweets
Miral al-Tahawy *Blue Aubergine • Brooklyn Heights • Gazelle Tracks • The Tent*
Bahaa Taher *As Doha Said • Love in Exile*
Fuad al-Takarli *The Long Way Back*
Zakaria Tamer *The Hedgehog*
M. M. Tawfik *candygirl • Murder in the Tower of Happiness*
Mahmoud Al-Wardani *Heads Ripe for Plucking*
Amina Zaydan *Red Wine*
Latifa al-Zayyat *The Open Door*